EMILY

Graham Duncanson

ISBN: 978-0-244-62986-1

Abbreviations

ADVS.	Assistant Director of Veterinary Services
CBPP	Contagious Bovine Pleural Pneumonia
DC	District Commissioner
DLO	District Livestock Officer
DO	District Officer
DVS	Director of Veterinary Services
FAO	Food and Agricultural Organisation
FMD	Foot and Mouth Disease
LMD	Livestock Marketing Division
NFD	Northern Frontier District
ODA	Overseas Development Agency
PM	Post Mortem
PPL	Private Pilot's License
PC	Provincial Commissioner

Chapter 1

Emily arrives in Kenya

Saturday 24th December 1966

Emily was devastated. She sat at the table on the veranda with her head in her hands. She was out of her depth. She was totally at a loss as to what to do. She wanted to weep, but knew that would show weakness. Abdi in his Kansu stood patiently in front of her. Slowly he tried his English,

"The Memsahib is dead. What are your orders?"

"Can you make some tea?" How she wished she could speak Swahili. Abdi nodded and turned towards the kitchen. Then she heard a radio crackle. Then she heard an English voice.

"This is PVO Coast calling all stations."

She thanked God. She could get advice. She had seen the Long Wave Radio (LWR) in her great aunt's bedroom. Then she realised that she had to face the body again. At least now Abdi had covered it with a sheet. She summoned up all her strength and went into the room.

You could hardly call it a room. Its walls were stretched tight hessian to a height of six feet. There was no door only a curtain of hessian. Her own bedroom, was slightly smaller, but otherwise was exactly the same. It was next door and she had only slept in it last night for the first time after her long exhausting journey in a lorry.

The radio was on a wooden table. There was a wooden chair in front of it. She could see two leads from it to a car battery on the floor. There was a black aerial cable going straight up through the palm thatch. Mercifully she knew how to work a radio. They had them in the vet's cars where she had seen veterinary practice, when she was a veterinary student.

Before she could sit down or do anything an Asian voice came on the air.

"PVO Coast, this is LO Lamu. 300 head of steers were mouthed and loaded on to Bonanza this morning. Bonanza left Mkowe at 7.00am."

"Well done, Happy Christmas. The next call will be the day after tomorrow."

An African voice came on the air before Emily could press the switch on her microphone.

"PVO Coast, this is LO Sabaki. All veterinary treatments were completed at Kurawa yesterday. Will return to Sabaki today and call the day after tomorrow." The English voice said,

"Happy Christmas, PVO Coast out." Emily was desperate. She pressed the microphone switch and forgot all the radio procedure.

"Help, it's Emily." The English voice replied,

"This is PVO Coast; your time is not for another twenty minutes." Emily was desperate,

"Please don't ring off. I'm all alone at Galana, Auntie Mary died in the night. I don't know what to do!" Mercifully the English voice answered,

"I'm so sorry to hear that Emily. I won't shut down. I assume Auntie Mary is Mary Barrington-Long. Was she ill?"

"No, she was fine last night. Abdi found her this morning, when he took in her tea. What should I do?" Emily hoped that she did not sound as desperate as she was. Equally she did want this calm guy to help her. If he was the Provincial Veterinary Officer, he must be very senior and he would take charge. The voice answered,

"I apologise for being so rude and trying to shut you up. I thought you must be one of the missionaries, who use this frequency after us. I have known your Auntie Mary for several years and because she was often alone, we had grown quite close. I know she had been suffering with heart problems for some months. She would have hated to been an invalid and in fact would have wanted to have gone this way. She always said she wanted to be buried on that hill on the southern end of the runway overlooking the Galana River. So if you can go with Abdi and select a place he can organise a grave to be dug. I will fly up her Doctor Ian Macleod for him to sign the death

2

certificate. We should be up with you in about an hour and a half."
Emily replied,

"Oh thank you. I feel so alone and hopeless. I can't even speak Swahili."

"OK. Can you get Abdi and help him with the radio? I will tell him what to do."

Emily got Abdi to the radio and she heard a fairly rapid exchange in Swahili and then the voice said,

"See you soon, Emily. Choose a spot with Abdi. PVO out."

Emily drank her tea and to her surprise, Abdi brought her a fried breakfast. She thought she wasn't hungry, but actually when she started to eat, because she thought it would be rude to Abdi if she didn't, she enjoyed her breakfast. Then the two of them set off walking the two hundred yards to the near end of the airstrip. There was indeed a small mound as the PVO had said. Abdi had brought a panga (An African Machete) and solemnly marked out the grave site. They walked back to the house, if you could call it that. Emily did her best and said,

"*Asante sana* (Thank you)." Abdi just nodded his head.

Emily went and sat on the veranda overlooking the river. She heard men's voices which she assumed was the grave digging party. She thought to herself. '*What a nightmare. I know I am tired from the long journey, but it does seem life has been cruel to me.*'

Emily came from a farming family in Kent. She had an elder brother who would take over the farm eventually from her father who was still very active. Emily had always wanted two things in life. She wanted to be a vet and she wanted to go to Africa.

It had been hard to get into veterinary college. She had been lucky and had got into Bristol which only admitted thirty students a year. Normally there would be only one or two girls, but she had been once again lucky, there were five other girls in her year. She had worked very hard at college, but she had also had a good time socially. She had graduated nearly at the top of her year.

Then rejection had started. There were jobs available through the Ministry of Overseas Development Administration (ODA) for newly qualified vets to go to work in many countries in Africa both as field vets or in laboratories. There were places at the School of Veterinary Tropical Medicine in Edinburgh for new graduates to study for a

3

year to obtain a Diploma in Veterinary Tropical Medicine. Emily filled out numerous application forms. She rarely got an interview. If she did, she was sure she was not considered, either because she was female, or because she was very small. She was 4ft 10 inches tall. In fact she was very strong for her weight. She was much stronger than many of the boys at college. She was also strikingly beautiful and therefore was not considered. Initially it made her very cross and then it just made her sad. She had little trouble getting locum jobs doing small animal veterinary work. She kept doing these jobs, as it improved her surgical skills and it also brought in money, so that she was totally independent from her family. She just could not get the job that she had set her heart on.

Then out of the blue her parents received a letter from her father's aunt in Kenya, saying she was suffering from a minor heart condition which her doctor thought was not serious. However he suggested that she employed a young person to help her on her ranch. Auntie Mary had heard that they had a daughter who had qualified as a vet. Auntie Mary wondered if their daughter would like to come out to Kenya at Auntie Mary's expense and work with her on her ranch which had over a thousand head of cattle. Emily jumped at the chance.

She had an up to date passport. She had to have several injections. Auntie Mary booked her flight from Heathrow to Embakasi. She said that Emily would arrive in the morning of the 23rd of December. Auntie Mary said she would arrange for transport to meet her at the airport. She said she would instruct her headman, Julius, to look out for Emily. Emily should wait at the airport until Julius found her.

Emily had never flown before. It was quite stressful getting to Heathrow. Once on the plane, Emily relaxed. She ate the supper that she was given. As she was offered a free small bottle of red wine she drank it. The plane was less than half full, so Emily saw other passengers stretching out on three adjoining seats and did the same. So in fact she did get several hours sleep. However her arrival was once again very stressful. She had put her 'Yellow Fever Vaccination Certificate' in a 'safe place'. She could not find it. She could feel the African official getting impatient. Then she could feel the whole queue getting cross. She tipped her whole handbag out on the floor, as there was no 'Health Examination Desk'. At last she found it, tucked in her passport. She just prayed that she had not lost anything vital out of her handbag. She stuffed everything back. At least she had her passport ready, when she got to immigration. Her passport was dully stamped.

Then she had to try and retrieve her suitcase. It was totally unsuitable, as it was very heavy to lift, but she did not own a rucksack and so she had borrowed the case from her parents. She had brought lots of her veterinary notes and some text-books which was why it was so heavy. She had the minimum amount of clothes. Her mother had made her bring a long dress, as her mother had said she thought some Kenya folk were very aristocratic and therefore she might get invited to a ball. Emily thought that was very unlikely, but she put the dress in to humour her mother. It was very light silk so compared to her text-books, it was nothing. She did not have any Kenyan money, so she did not want a porter, as she could not pay him. She found her bag and then humped it, with difficulty on to an airport trolley. She was frightened that she was going to have her handbag stolen and then she would be in a real muddle. She wheeled the trolley over to Customs. A man in uniform insisted that she put the case on to a table. That was a mission. He then insisted the case was opened. All her clothes burst out. The Customs man made a perfunctory examination of her clothes and then said she could close it again. Emily then really struggled to get the locks to click into place; she was nearly in tears, when at last she managed it. She was the last to leave the Customs hall. Outside there were several taxi drivers who all wanted to take her into Nairobi. She was at her wits end, when a wizened old man came up to her and said,

"Memsahib. I am Julius. You stay here. I send men for your case."

Once again Emily was on her own thinking, '*when will this nightmare ever end.*' Suddenly two enormous Africans were by her side. One hoisted the case on to his head. She thought for one dreadful moment that the second man was going to hoist her on to his head and carry her out of the airport. Mercifully he just indicated that she should stay close behind him and he pushed his way through the crowd. Outside there was still a frantic bustle, but this enormous man guided her though the crowd which melted away, as they came to a big lorry filled with stores on which sat about twenty more enormous men.

Emily was ushered into the cab of lorry. In the driver's seat was a grinning man, who said,

"I am the driver. My name is Christmas." Julius then got in beside her and they set off. Emily thanked Julius and Christmas for picking her up. She prayed that her case had gone on the lorry. She soon realised that they spoke very little English. There was silence in the cab. She was amazed that she suddenly saw a herd of zebra on her right and in the distance she could make out giraffe. She smiled to herself. She had got one of her wishes. She had arrived in Africa.

The lorry carried on down the Tarmac road for nearly three hours. Emily was bursting for a wee, when at last they stopped at a Shell garage, called 'Hunter's Lodge'. She scampered to a lavatory behind the garage. She was petrified they would leave without her. The lavatory was filthy, but she was so glad she had made it without wetting herself.

When she got back to the lorry, they had filled up and we're ready to go. Julius had bought her a cold coke and a pastry parcel called a samosa, containing very spicy minced beef. It was very tasty. Emily was grateful. However the Tarmac had ended and they ploughed on, on a red 'murram' road. Red dust filled the cab. It got everywhere. When they stopped at a garage for more fuel at Voi, a hundred miles further on from Hunter's Lodge, Emily was appalled that her knickers were red with dust. She consoled herself with the fact that she had seen so much game on the way, elephant, warthogs and baboons. This was the real Africa of her dreams, even though she was in a hot dusty cab of an old lorry.

Fifty miles past Voi, they at last came to more Tarmac at Mackinnon Road. However almost immediately they turned left back on to a red murram road which Julius tried to explain was a fire-break on the edge of Tsavo East Game Park and was used by Galana ranch as a stock-route to bring their cattle to the railway station at Mackinnon Road. It began getting dark and Emily saw even more game, when Christmas turned on the headlights of the lorry. This so called fire-break was very rough, so not only was their speed reduced, but also the lorry bucked about throwing Emily on to either Julius or Christmas. Neither of them seemed bothered and so Emily assumed that this was what was expected. It was totally dark, when Christmas slowed the lorry. There in the headlights was a wide red river, The Galana. To Emily's horror Julius told her that all of them except two guards would have to wade across. He suggested that she waded across with her handbag on her head. He would get one of the men to bring her suitcase.

Emily was a brave girl, but her courage nearly deserted her. Were there crocodiles in the river? How deep was it? Would she be washed away and drown? She was a good swimmer, but in her clothes and holding her handbag she lost all her confidence. Julius saw her hesitate and offered to take her handbag. Emily did not want to lose face, so she said very bravely, I will be fine. Keeping her trainers on she took off her shirt and trousers and pushed them into her handbag which was like a large snake basket. Then she set off in her bra and kickers after Julius. Even though she was short she was relieved that the water did not come above breasts. She was glad that she had kept her trainers on as, although initially it was muddy, as she entered the river, it soon had a rocky bottom. She fought from thinking about the murky red water and what it contained. Christmas had kept the engine of the lorry running, so that the swirling waters were illuminated in the lights. She kept her eyes focused on Julius and just followed him. She could hear the voices of the other men behind her. Mercifully the river stayed at the same depth. It was not cold, but because she was so frightened she kept shivering.

Emily had always had a good sense of balance and so she did not slip, as she slowly made her way across the river with her handbag on her head. At last Julius reached the far bank and started to climb up the crude rock stairway out of the river. Immediately as Emily came out of the water she felt really cold, as the air temperature was lower than that of the water. However the exertion soon warmed her up, as did the sense of achievement. Then suddenly she felt shy illuminated by the lights of the truck just dressed in her bra and knickers. She stopped to put on her shirt and trousers. The men behind patiently waited. Then she moved quickly to catch up Julius. Once he had climbed up the bank he had set off on a well trodden path running beside the river.

Soon there were lights ahead and voices. They were obviously expected. After a further few minutes they started to climb again but this time on proper concrete steps. There was Auntie Mary.

"Hello Emily, Dear. You poor girl! I had hoped you would get here in daylight. It's not actually late. I will show you the shower. There is lovely hot water to wash away the dirt of the river and the journey. I will find you a bathrobe for you to wear for supper. Abdi will take away your wet clothes."

Emily found it was rather difficult to see as the hurricane lamps were not very bright. There did not seem to be a door to the shower, only a very flimsy hessian curtain. Emily felt she was giving everyone a wonderful view as she washed herself gratefully in the warm water of the shower. She knew her fine fair hair would soon dry in the warm wind. She found the bathrobe which was not really too big for her. Auntie Mary was short like her.

Emily was hungry and she soon demolished the chilli cone carne which was followed by lovely fresh pineapple. She listened as Auntie Mary told her all about the ranch. Apparently the million and a half acres were not owned by Auntie Mary, but was a concession from the government. Auntie Mary owned all the equipment and more importantly all the cattle. She had mobs of breeding cows, groups of stock bulls and other mobs of younger stock. The steers and the less well bred heifers were destined for slaughter. The better heifers were destined to be mated and join the breeding herd. There seemed to be hundreds of staff, including an old European, Colin Roberts, who was away with his niece in Nairobi for Christmas. He was due back on the 31st of December. He lived in a similar house to this, about half a mile away down the river. Apparently you could actually drive to the ranch, but it was a very long way on a very rough road inland from the coast, north of the Sabaki Bridge which was north of Malindi. If Emily had come in that way it would have added another two hundred miles to her journey. Wading across the Galana River, which turned into the Sabaki as it got nearer to the coast was much easier.

"Next time My Dear, you must wade across in your swim-suit. I know the Giriama ladies at the coast walk around bare-chested, but I think it is important that us Europeans set a good example and are properly dressed. Of course there was no need for you to come across fully clothed!"

"I'm sorry Auntie Mary. I did not realise and I came across in my bra and pants."

"Don't worry my Dear. I'm sure you were perfectly decent."

After a good cup of coffee they both went to bed. Emily found her case in her room. Miraculously it had not been dropped in the river, but it did smell very fishy. She found her pyjamas and slept like a log until Abdi woke her with the tragic news in the morning.

Chapter 2

Help Arrives

Mid-morning Saturday 24th December 1966

Emily kept herself busy while she was waiting for the plane. She totally unpacked her case. She hung up her clothes on a rail, there was no wardrobe. She looked at the long black evening dress with sadness and thought there is no possible chance I will wear this. However she had made it to Africa and she was sure with all these cattle there was going to be a lot of veterinary work which she would find exciting. She was just going to be very lonely. She was not a racist, but she knew that her culture was widely removed from all the Kenyan Staff. She vowed to learn Swahili as quick as she could. She found, 'Teach Yourself Swahili' as she was stacking her text-books on the book shelves in the living room which in fact was just an enormous veranda over-looking the river. The two bedrooms and bathrooms were behind it. There was a big table on the veranda which was also the dining room. The kitchen was separated from the house by about ten yards. There was a covered walk-way to it behind the house. Nothing was at all private. The bathrooms were only separate from the walk-way by the thin stretched hessian.

Abdi had only just brought her a cup of coffee, when she heard the plane. It came from the south, flew over the house and then must have turned out of her view and landed. She could not stop herself. She ran to the airstrip. The plane was tiny. As it taxied up to her, she got covered in red dust. When the engine stopped, two very serious men got out of the plane. The younger who she estimated was in his late twenties strode quickly towards her. He opened his arms to her. She could not stop. She burst into tears and hugged him, as if he was the last person on earth. She thought he must be the doctor and the other old man was the senior vet, the PVO. The younger man stroked her hair and soothed her saying,

"You poor girl, you mustn't cry we are here to support you. Mary would have wanted to go quickly; she would have hated to be an invalid. I am Simon Longfield and this is Doctor Ian Macleod."

Emily then realised that the old man was the doctor and this young guy was the PVO. However was he so senior? She suddenly remembered her manners and sprang away from his arms. They had felt so strong and comforting. She remembered Simon's lovely kind eyes. She shook hands with Ian. She led them on a solemn journey down to the house. Abdi had already brought more coffee and biscuits.

However she turned to Ian and said,

"Before you sit down to coffee would you like to see Auntie Mary?" He replied,

"Yes that would be sensible." As she led him into the bedroom she said,

"There is soap and a towel in the bathroom next door. I will leave you. I did not know Auntie Mary well, but I would rather remember her as she was last night talking and laughing than lying dead." Ian was obviously a kind old man. He replied,

"Of course I understand. You go and keep Simon company. I will soon join you for coffee."

Simon was standing on the edge of the veranda, holding his coffee looking at the river. Emily longed for him to put his arm around her again, as she stood beside him. He said,

"This is the real Africa. It is very beautiful, but I imagine it makes you sad having only just arrived. Where's Colin? I hope he is helping you."

"He is away until New Years Eve, with his niece in Nairobi. I haven't met him yet. What's he like?" Simon turned and she wanted to melt into those smiling brown eyes.

"He is a kind experienced rancher who was devoted to Mary, as she employed him, when his ranching enterprise went bust after four years of drought. Sadly he is rather taciturn, so I think you will find it hard learning from him. I have been rather brutally honest, but I did not want to build up your hopes. I feel sad for you on your own up here for Christmas. All my family are in England, so I have spent a

Christmas up here when Mary took some leave. I know what it is like. It is difficult for me. I don't want to push myself on to you, but would you like me to stay for the two days of the holiday while you settle in? I assume you are going to stay?" Emily could not stop being eager,

"Oh please stay. I would so love that. You are so senior would you be allowed to be away from Mombasa?" Simon laughed,

"I'm not that senior! It is just that I arrived out here at the right time before the Kenyan vets had graduated from Nairobi. I'm in charge of the Coast and North Eastern Provinces. I'm really free to be anywhere within them. Officially I should get permission to leave them from the Director of Veterinary Services (DVS). However things are pretty lax. I don't think he minds, when I go away to play rugby or go sailing at weekends provided I'm contactable. He certainly would not mind if I was up here making myself useful."

"Thank you. That would be so kind of you. I will try and entertain you." Then Emily laughed,

"That sounds bad doesn't it? I didn't mean to say quite that." She was saved further embarrassment by Ian coming on to the veranda. She offered him some coffee and asked,

"Doctor Macleod what is the form now?"

Ian looked at Simon. Emily thought Simon was so marvellous. He was much the younger man, but he immediately took charge. Simon turned to her and said,

"Obviously it is entirely up to you, but what I would suggest is that Abdi and the domestic staff wrap Mary in a tarpaulin to act as a shroud and then they carry her up to the grave that Abdi has had dug. They lay her in the grave. I will read the short Anglican burial service. You instruct Julius that any of the farm staff may attend. That will start stamping your authority here on Galana. Later you can look through her papers and see if you can find a will. I will fly Ian back to Mombasa and then return by air." Emily just nodded her head and said,

"Thank you Simon that is what we will do."

The small burial was really quite moving. Emily openly wept, but she wasn't embarrassed. Simon put his arm around her at the grave, as she threw in the first soil on to the tarpaulin. Then she walked away on her own to the river, while the grave was filled in. She returned to thank Ian and say goodbye. She kissed Simon on the cheek saying,

"Have a safe flight." Then she cried again saying,

"You are all I have in the world for ten thousand miles." Simon replied,

"You may be very surprised, Mary was rather special. I think the staff here will be very loyal to you. We will have a memorial service for her in Mombasa at some stage. I took the liberty of putting an announcement in the Daily Nation."

Then he got into the plane with Ian, and shouted, "Prop clear." He taxied away to take off.

Emily dried her eyes and made her way back to what she was now going to call home. She started going through Auntie Mary's desk, to look for her will. Uninstructed Abdi made her some lunch of cold ham, tomatoes, sweet corn and mashed potatoes, followed by mangos. He indicated that Simon had told him that he was returning later, so Emily was relieved that she did not have to give Abdi any instructions about supper or making up a bed. She assumed that Simon would not mind using Auntie Mary's room.

Emily could not find Auntie Mary's will in the desk. However she did find a key in the top draw. She showed it to Abdi. He led her into Auntie Mary's room and showed her the gun safe which was set in the concrete under her bed. The key fitted the safe which contained a twelve bore shot gun, a .22 rifle and a bundle of papers. The bundle among other things contained her will. It was very simple and had been made recently after Emily had agreed to come to Kenya. There was a list of her staff with small legacies starting with the largest to Abdi and Julius with decreasing amounts to them all. There was a legacy of £5000 to Colin Roberts and the rest of her estate was bequeathed to Emily. A firm of solicitors in Mombasa were her authorised executors. Emily was gobsmacked. It made her a very wealthy woman. Emily cried as Auntie Mary had written how proud she was of Emily for becoming a vet, something she had always wished to become. Emily returned the bundle of papers to the safe. The key to the safe was not large and so Emily put it on the gold chain she always wore around her neck.

She heard Simon return. This time she tried to be more demure and she walked casually up to the airstrip. She found Simon tying the plane to three heavy blocks of concrete. Simon explained that as the plane which was called a 'Piper Colt' was a very light, high-winged plane, it was safer to tie it down in case a high wind got up and damaged it. They walked to the house chatting. Simon carried a rucksack and a grip together with a canvass gun sleeve. He said he had brought very little except for some basic veterinary gear and his shot gun. Luckily he was carrying things in both hands or Emily was sure she would have reached up to hold his hand. He was a giant compared to her. She was so pleased to see him. She had been so depressed with her tiring journey and the death of her aunt. It was Christmas Eve and now she was really looking forward to Christmas. Conversation came very easy to both of them. She told him about her home and her time at college. He told her about his life out here. What really pleased her was that he was very enthusiastic about the development of her as a veterinary surgeon. All her worries about rejection because she was small and a girl were forgotten. He made her laugh by reminding her that 'A strong woman is a lot better than a weak man'. She loved it that he was so polite to Abdi and the staff. Over the meal he started to teach her some Swahili. He was impressed with her memory. He rarely had to repeat a word. She remembered them all. She even made Abdi laugh with her Swahili, when he came to say good night.

It might have been very inconvenient not having electricity, but it was very romantic. There was no embarrassment, when it was time to go to bed. They both could hear each other in the shower and on the loo. In fact when Simon had got into bed under his mosquito-net he called out to her,

"Goodnight, sleep well. I will test you on your Swahili at breakfast." Then he chuckled. Emily hugged herself. She thought he was so lovely. She wondered if there was a woman in his life. She could not believe that there wasn't."

Obviously it was business as normal in the morning. Abdi brought them tea soon after day break which came quickly, as they were not far south of the equator. Simon called out,

"*Habari asabui* (Good morning how are you)". She was proud to reply,

"*Mzuri sana, Habari aki* (Very well, how are you). She wanted to hug him, when they both parted their hessian curtains together. He upstaged her as he lent forward and kissed her on the cheek saying,

"Happy Christmas." Emily said,

"My goodness I had totally forgotten. Happy Christmas." She felt him draw back slightly when she hugged him. Obviously she had gone a bit too far. However they were soon chatting away over the good breakfast which Abdi had provided.

They arranged with Abdi the time for lunch. It was a good learning experience as 12 noon was *sa sita* (literately six o'clock in Swahili). Emily would have got in a real muddle, if Simon had not explained that 7 o'clock in the morning was *sa mojo asabui* (meaning the first hour of the day). They first had a good look around the house. Emily could see how she had got such lovely hot water. It was a very simple system. A little boy, called Johno, had to keep a fire going under a 44 gallon drum fixed to the hot pipes. He also did the laundry.

Simon made her laugh by telling her about long-drops and how lucky she was to have a flushing toilet with a seat rather than a hole in the ground.

They walked up to the airstrip to make sure the plane was OK. Then they walked to the dairy boma which was nearby. Two cows were milked for the house and, for the house and office staff. Apparently each mob of cattle had one or two milk cattle to provide milk for the herdsmen. They inspected the nearest spray race, where the cattle were sprayed weekly to prevent tick infestation which spread several diseases. Emily made Simon promise to tell her more about these diseases, when they got back, so that she could take notes. He seemed to have such a wealth of information. He was much more knowledgeable than the lecturers at college. They climbed a nearby hill with a tank on top. Simon explained how the water was pumped up from wells near to the river to this tank and then fed to the house and offices by gravity. In this way the pumps only needed to work for a few hours every day and not for the full 24 hours. They walked back to the house. Emily so wanted to hold his hand, but she knew she mustn't. She was very conscious that she would frighten him away if she was too possessive. It was just so lovely having him here. She dreaded when he would leave after the holiday.

Abdi did them proud for Christmas lunch. Simon had brought a frozen chicken from his deep freeze which was roasted with stuffing. There was even bread sauce and cranberry jelly. Emily was delighted as Simon had brought two crackers for them to pull. They only had water to drink as they had decided to go in one of the ranch Landrovers in the afternoon to see some of the cattle further from the house. Simon said he hoped he could shoot a Guinea fowl for their lunch the next day. Emily was amazed that there was a fridge which kept things cold by burning paraffin. Simon teased her, saying she surely was not that old that she had forgotten her 'O' level physics. Emily was also delighted as she realised that he was actually planning to stay for three whole days and three nights and only go back early in the morning on the second day after boxing day. She was pleased as Simon suggested that she should tell Abdi that as it was Christmas Day that they would get their own supper. What pleased her most was that when they went to get in the Landrover, he made her drive. It was such a little thing, but it made her feel valued. So many men recently had been trying to put her down. Simon was so different he encouraged her.

That night supper was even more romantic without Abdi. The hurricane lights guttered. There were insects trying to commit suicide, but mercifully there were no mosquitoes, just a few midges. Simon had some midge repellent. They both had a couple of beers and a glass of 'Amarula' with their coffee. Emily knew in her heart it would be naughty, but she also knew if he came into her bed she certainly would not stop him. In fact she knew she would encourage him. However in fact to her regret he behaved impeccably. They did not kiss, but he called out to her to sleep well. She called back to thank him for a lovely Christmas. Emily did not go to sleep instantly, as she was thinking about what it would feel like to be lying in his arms. Eventually she dropped off and slept soundly and only woke when Abdi brought her tea. She was dying to take her tea into Simon's room and join him in bed, but she was frightened of rejection. She did not want to spoil their relationship. She wished she had some sexy pyjamas and then she would have gone and looked at the river in the dawn and hoped that he would join her. However as it

16

was, she stole a few extra minutes in bed hoping he would come and join her. He didn't, but she heard him get up and she joined him at the breakfast table. He seemed in a very happy mood. In fact she could not remember him not in a happy mood except when they buried Auntie Mary. They were like old friends happy to see each other and be in each other's company. In the middle of breakfast he looked at his watch and said,

"Would you like to join me on the radio call?" He put his arm around her shoulders and gave her a little squeeze.

"Your use of the radio leaves a little to be desired! However it will be great to be able to communicate every day. We can make our own little code, as obviously anyone can listen in. Officially the Livestock Marketing Division (LMD) comes on first for thirty minutes, then the Coast Province and finally the missionaries. Because I used to work for the LMD and because a lot of the Coast traffic concerns the LMD we tend to work together." He laughed then and said,

"It is the missionaries who seem to rabbit on! I suggest you come in anytime when we are on. Auntie Mary has two radios, the one in my room and another one which officially is Galana mobile. I suggest you take it whenever you are going far away on the ranch, so you can call up if you get a break down."

He offered her the chair in front of the radio and drew up another next to it. Emily loved it that they were so close. She liked it even more when he said with a cheeky grin. I will imagine you sleeping in, and getting to the radio all tousled in you pyjamas. Emily could not resist it and said,

"What if I have just got out of the shower?" He laughed,

"I will go very red and start to stammer!" She replied,

"I will enjoy your discomfiture and then get all embarrassed if Abdi comes in to get the tea mug."

"That will really frighten, Abdi!"

Emily wondered if this conversation had made him as hot as she suddenly was. There were only short conversations on the radio and with reluctance Emily got up to return to the breakfast table. She felt so aroused she wished she could sit on his knee, but instead she had to make do with sitting next to him looking at the majestic, timeless, river.

As they were eating Simon told her about the coastal stock route. Emily was delighted, as he said the Auntie Mary had been very happy for him to plan to make a new stock route from Galole on the Tana river down her boundary to where they were now, so that LMD cattle could use the stock route on the other side of the river which Emily had driven up on her first day. Emily asked if the cattle had to wade across like she did. Simon said at the moment they would, but that he and Auntie Mary had planned to make a concrete causeway to make it easier for the cattle and to get stores and vehicles across. It was Emily's turn to laugh,

"That will be good. When I first arrived, I did not know the form so I took off my shirt and trousers and went across in my bra and knickers. Auntie Mary said it would more fitting if I had crossed in a swim suit as she said, although the Giriama ladies went bare-chested on the coast, we should set a good example. I would not have been worried if I was naked. I was just worried about crocodiles! Simon smiled,

"So if I want you to take your clothes off, I have got to find you a river with hungry crocs!" Emily replied,

"You watch it, Longfield!"

She thought, '*I would willingly take my clothes off for you.*' Then she thought, '*Actually I would be very shy.*'

They had an enjoyable day together exploring the nearer areas of the ranch. Obviously it was so vast they only saw a very small percentage of it. Simon shot a Yellow Necked Francolin for their supper. They visited the house, where Colin Roberts lived. It was similar to the main house. It had a high thatched '*Makuti*' roof with hessian walls. Everything appeared to be in order. His cook welcomed them and made them a cup of coffee. Emily was amazed that because they were Europeans he ushered them in, even though he had never met them before.

Emily was a little sad at supper as she knew that Simon had to leave early in the morning to get back to work. He wanted to get back to his office and carry out the radio call from there. Luckily his office was on the way from the airport on the causeway before Mombasa island so he would have no problem with the traffic. After Abdi had cleared away supper and had received his orders for the early start, they took their coffees and sat looking at the river in the moonlight. Emily so wanted to at least hold his hand, but she thought she should leave the first move to him. She wondered if they would go to bed together, but eventually Simon sighed and after moaning about the early start in the morning they went to their separate rooms. Emily lay awake, not only thinking about Simon in the next door room, but also worrying about the following night, when she was all alone.

At breakfast before dawn, Emily was delighted that Simon suggested that they turned their radios on at 8 pm so that she could let him know that all was well. At least she thought she would have some contact in this remote place. She walked with him in the semi-darkness to the airstrip. As normal in the tropics the dawn came very quickly. Simon gave her a quick hug, got in the plane and taxied away down the runway. She only cried when she thought he could not see. However he did see, as he took off. It broke his heart.

He was not sure why he was holding her at a distance. He found her very attractive. She was very mature and good fun. She made him laugh. Time with her flew by. He thought his main problem was that he felt desperately sorry for her and he thought that was not a good reason to start a relationship. He was so worried that if there was anything physical between them that it would all go wrong and ruin their friendship. His mind was in turmoil, as he sped in the air to Mombasa. The journey only took a little over half an hour. Even if he had driven the quicker route by wading across the river, the driving time would be well over four hours.

Emily listened in on the radio call up. She was dying to say something to him at the end, but kept her silence. What was there for her to say? 'I miss you so much already. When can we see each other again?' It sounded so childish even to her. To anyone listening it would sound totally puerile. She was sure it would embarrass him. She had only just met him. She dreaded driving him away. She so yearned for him. It was ridiculous. She just had to 'man up'.

When he said, "PVO Coast out," she could not stop herself pressing the microphone switch once. She was sure he had heard her, as she heard the double click of another microphone. She gulped back tears, turned off the radio and went to find Julius for his morning report.

She tried to keep busy during the day, but often she caught herself dreaming about Simon. It was strange. There was a large mass of work she could do on the ranch, but equally Auntie Mary had the staff very well trained and the day to day running was very efficient. Julius reported that he had replaced the nozzles on one spray race. All Emily had to do was to put that on a list to order from Nairobi to come with Colin Roberts on New Year's Eve. It seemed as if most things came from Nairobi even though Mombasa was nearer and in theory everything which was imported came through the Port of Mombasa.

She had an early supper before it was dark. Time dragged then until 8 pm. She tried to make an order for all the veterinary equipment which she should have. She and Simon had discussed it at length. Still 8 pm did not come.

When at last it did come, Emily was so grateful that Simon came on exactly on time. However she was sad as it was a very stilted conversation. Whether it was because they were conscious that the whole world could be listening or because they had nothing more to say to each other, Emily did not know. It seemed to make her sadder, as she sensed that Simon was not happy. He ended rather abruptly saying they would speak tomorrow. Emily realised as probably they both realised that unless they had anything specific to say the radio was not a good idea.

She was very lonely as she went to bed. She realised this was actually the first night she had actually been alone. She wept when she thought of Auntie Mary who had at least been alive, when she went to bed on her first night.

As she lay in bed failing to sleep she chastised herself. She wasn't alone, there were over a hundred staff probably within shouting distance. She had got her two wishes; she was in Africa, it was real Africa not some package tour in a game sanctuary surrounded by a fence and she had employment.

She was sure she was going to get a lot of veterinary work, not only because of all the cattle on the ranch, but also because Simon had told her there was a definite shortage of vets. Her small animal experience would come in useful.

Also she was astute enough to realise that even if she sold up everything on the ranch tomorrow she would be a wealthy woman. If she carried on ranching she could potentially become a very wealthy woman.

She flopped on to her back and thought about Simon. He was so lovely and kind. She knew even if their relationship came to nothing, he would be a great teacher. With the thought of her arms wrapped around him, she slept. She was still asleep at day break when Abdi brought the tea. She quickly showered and dressed. She told Abdi she would be back in for breakfast after the radio call. She went to find Julius for him to brief her on what was happening on the ranch.

She was pleased that there had been no disasters. Lion attack was always a danger. She knew Julius would advise her, but she would have liked Simon's advice as well.

She wondered what Colin Roberts was going to be like. She had already noticed that the records were a complete mess. Her project at college had been based on improving records in a large beef herd to improve productivity. She was sure she could use this knowledge to good effect.

She also was interested in finance, as her father had encouraged her to help as a farm secretary and do his farm books. She knew this would be a help. She rightly guessed that if she took on these two aspects of the ranch she could improve things radically without stepping on Colin's toes. The veterinary cupboard was a total jumble.

She vowed to take this on whether Colin or Julius liked it or not. She was sure Auntie Mary had her in mind for this roll.

In the farm office she found meticulous records about the vehicles, water pumps and spray-races. They were not in Auntie Mary's hand writing. Obviously it could have been an African who was away on leave. She asked Julius. He confirmed what she had suspected that this was Colin's doing.

In the same hand writing was all the staff records, pay, leave, increments etc. Emily was pleased as she certainly didn't want that job.

She was so busy that she was slightly late for the radio call. She guessed that Simon had not used her call sign as right at the end she heard his voice which sounded concerned. "Galana base this is PVO Coast, over." She immediately responded,

"PVO Coast this is Galana base. All well here."

"Glad to hear that Galana base. We will speak tomorrow morning. I will do some investigating to see if we could get some link set up so that I can at least give you some more urgent verbal support if you need it. I had forgotten to tell you that I can pick up this frequency in an airplane if I am airborne in quite a large area of the Coast Province, particularly if I'm at altitude. If you listen to the normal morning call, you will hear any plans which have been made for me. Take Care. PVO Coast over and out."

Emily thought, well at least he is thinking about me. He can't say more over the radio than, 'Take Care'. Abdi came in with her fried breakfast which she cheerfully ate.

Chapter 3

New Year's Night

Saturday 31st December 1966

For the next few days she and Simon acknowledged each other on the radio, but did not chat. After the morning call on the 31st December, when Simon said he would not be on the radio on the 1st, she was really miserable. However she made herself busy and the morning went quickly. After lunch the day dragged. Emily thought she had never had a New Years Night, when she had not been celebrating with somebody.

She came in at 3.30 pm for a cup of tea. Then she heard an airplane. Could it be Simon? Anyhow at least it was someone. She ran to the airstrip. It was him. She recognised the plane. She had to stop herself from flinging her arms around him. He had a big smile on his face.

"I funked asking you for a date on the radio, but would you like to come to a dinner-dance in Mombasa? You could stay over and I could fly you back tomorrow."

"I would love that. Come in for a cup of tea while I get some clothes together. Is it long or short dresses?"

"Long I think. Yes a cuppa would be good. I will brief Abdi, so he knows what's happening."

"Long suits me. I haven't really got a smart short dress. I'm getting on really well with my Swahili. Abdi actually understands a lot of English."

They walked to the house in companionable silence. Emily had found a rucksack two days ago in the farm office. She threw in stuff which she thought she would need. She was on top of the world. She came through and thanked Abdi for the tea. He had also made a cake which Simon devoured with relish. Then they were off. Simon talked her through the flying. He made hold the stick and have her feet on the pedals, so she could follow what he was doing. The plane was quite noisy so they had to shout. Emily loved the flying. It was over too quickly. However she also loved driving with him from the airport to his house. It was enormous. He showed her to her room which was upstairs and had a beautiful view of Tudor Creek. She had her own bathroom. She had a lovely shower with the fan going in both the bathroom and the bedroom to keep her cool. It was only when she put on her dress that she realised she had problems. She called to Simon who she guessed was in the opposite room to hers, also off the veranda.

"Have you got a needle and some black cotton? I have only got flat black shoes and the dress is made for high heels."

"Not a problem. Jonathan, my cook will help. He does all my mending. Bring the dress and the shoes so you can show him how much to turn up. I will come down with you."

Emily was dully introduced to Jonathan. Although he only spoke Swahili, he immediately saw the problem. He made Simon hold the dress up and he put pins where he was going to turn it up. Luckily Emily had put on a pair of shorts and a shirt; otherwise she would have been sitting around in her bra and knickers. Simon put on his Dinner Jacket and got them some G & Ts. Emily was amazed how quickly Jonathan did the job. He said something in Swahili, as he gave the dress back. Emily did not understand, but she was sure he meant, 'Have good evening'. Simon told her the 'Chini Club' where they were going was virtually next door so they could easily walk, when she was ready. When she came back on the veranda he said,

"Wow, you look sensational. Thank you so much for coming. So often at these dos it is all couples. It is boy girl, boy girl, Simon, boy girl etc." Emily laughed,

"I bet you have lots of girl friends!" Simon replied,

"I don't know about lots. There have been a few. Kenya is a favourite destination to come too, for girls from the UK."

They finished their G & Ts and walked down to the Mombasa club which was called the 'Chini Club' meaning below in Swahili. It was very smart, but old fashioned. Simon was not actually a member as he belonged to the Mombasa Sports club where he played rugger and squash. He was allowed into the Mombasa Club because he was a member of the Nanuyki Sports Club which had reciprocal arrangements with the Mombasa Club. They were met by the rather pompous club secretary who insisted that Emily was 'signed in'. Emily was not fazed by this, as she was used to the rather old fashion behaviour of the hall of residence, when she was at veterinary college. She slipped her arm through Simon's and they went down stairs to the large dining room all decorated for Christmas. Simon saw their table and led her across. They were the last to arrive. The other eight couples immediately got up. Emily felt the appraising looks from them all, mainly from the other girls. Silently she thanked her mother for insisting she brought this long dress. Whether it was because she was with Simon and he had been so complimentary, or because she knew the dress fitted her well and suited her, she felt on top of the world. This feeling was soon dashed by Eve who was married to Richard who was a doctor, she said,

"Are you flying for British Overseas Airways?" Simon immediately said quite sharply,

"No she does not. She is a vet like me." Emily was very grateful to him particularly as another man, called Fred who was married to Sylvia and was in 'shipping' said.

"I imagine you deal with cats and dogs as you are so petite" Emily did her best to smile as although it might have been a compliment, she thought it was rather rude. He went on by saying, 'You would never have the strength to deliver a calf.' Emily was not going to take that. She looked him in the eye and said,

"A strong woman is much better than a weak man."

An older lady, who was called Betty and was married to Jack, said they were ranchers from Voi which Emily remembered from her journey down to Galana. Betty added,

"Well said my dear. You must move with the times Fred. I hear there are more girl vets now. Jack and I will be delighted if you can come and see our cattle." Emily was really grateful to her. Emily could tell this was not going to be an easy evening, particularly as the last lady that she was introduced to, called Cynthia, obviously fancied Simon and hardly bother to say hello. Her husband, Mike was more jovial. He owned a farm and a butcher's shop. Emily sat next to Mike. Simon was on her other side. Emily noticed that

Cynthia managed to arrange it so she was sitting on Simon's other side. The food seemed marvellous to Emily, but the other ladies found fault with it.

Although Cynthia tried her very best to keep Simon's attention, Emily was so grateful that he kept returning to her. With more drink the table became more relaxed. Emily thought to herself. There was I feeling lonely and sorry for myself at Galana, but in reality if Simon was not here, I would hate this. She was pleased when the meal was over and the disco started. Emily loved dancing and in fact could jive really well. She and Simon got the dancing going. They did not seem to try that hard but they somehow always seemed to know what they each were going to do. When they eventually sat down at the table, Simon said,

"That was good fun. You are a great dancer." Then he lent forward and whispered in her ear,

"Make sure you save the last dance for me?" Emily whispered, with a smile,

"Are you worried that Cynthia might eat you?" He whispered back,

"Yes, something like that."

Emily danced with all the men on their table. Mike got so red in the face that she thought he was going to have a heart attack. She and Jack had a very sedate dance. He stressed to her that she must come to Voi. She promised she would. Emily found she liked Richard. He was Ian's younger partner. When she said how grateful she was to Ian for being so kind after Auntie Mary's death. Richard suddenly realised who she was and he laughed.

"You must forgive my wife. She thinks all good looking girls are air hostesses. She chooses to forget she was one and met me out here when she was on a crew stop-over." His hand dropped on to Emily's bottom. She moved further away from him as they danced. She made a mental note to register with Ian. She certainly did not want Richard to be her doctor.

It was getting near to midnight and Simon made sure he was dancing with Emily. It was a waltz. Emily felt him draw her close. She thought she would risk putting both arms around his neck. She was so relieved he didn't seem to mind. As midnight came she was in ecstasy as he kissed her. She noticed Cynthia and Eve made a big deal of kissing him. They all sang 'Auld Lang Syne' and then the party was over. The others tried to encourage Simon and Emily to have a last drink, but they ducked out and walked home. Emily held his hand once they were away from the others. It was so beautiful in the moonlight with the creek, black on their left. To Emily's eyes there seemed even more stars than at Galana. They came to the house which was in darkness, the moon gave them enough light to see; now they had some night vision. Simon said, as he turned on the small light on the table on the veranda,

"I forgot to give you your 'Happy New Year' present. I did not have time for a present at Christmas." He gave her a small soft parcel wrapped in brown paper. Emily was so touched she almost cried, but managed,

"Oh Simon, thank you."

She undid the parcel. It was a bright, pretty, orange kikoi which Emily knew most Kenyan people used as pyjamas. Hers were so hot, but she wore them because she was often asleep, when Abdi brought in her early morning cup of tea. She exclaimed,

"Simon it is so pretty. I am always too hot in my pyjamas."

As she opened the kikoi, two brown bits of cloth fell out. It was a bikini. Simon said rather hesitantly,

"I hope it fits. I know it is not an appropriate thing for me to buy as a present. It is rather a dull colour, but I hope it will be useful if we go on safari in the hot, NFD." He added, "How silly of me you will be used to the heat, unlike other girls, as you live in the NFD!"

"Simon thank you, a thousand thanks." She wrapped her arms around him and would have kissed him passionately, but she sensed him stiffen and stopped. She said very seriously,

"I have not got a present for you. I only have my body which I will wrap in my lovely new kikoi!"

Simon looked down at her,

"Your body is the best present that I have ever been given, but you know nothing about me. Come let's sit in the moonlight?"

She sat on his knee with her arm around his neck. Simon said,

"Emily, you have no idea how much I want you, but I know I mustn't touch you. I have been a bad boy. I think my Grandmother would say I am a 'Rake'. You are so kind and gentle it would not be right for you to go with me. I know I will hurt you."

27

"Simon you don't know that I'm not the female equivalent of a rake. I think my Grandmother would say a girl of easy virtue or my brother would say the 'local bike'!"

"Emily, I just know you are not."

"No I'm not. I got very friendly with a guy two years ahead of me at college. We broke up, when he qualified and went to work in the Lake District. I was sad, but in some way relieved, as I knew in my heart he was not the man for me. My guess is you have had a fling with both Cynthia and Eve?"

"I'm sorry Emily there have been many others. I really want us, to be friends. I so want to help you at Galana and out here in Kenya. We will just have to keep some distance between us. My guess is you have decided to run Galana in Mary's memory?"

"You are right. I was amazed that she virtually left the whole ranch to me and she hardly knew me."

"She might not have known you very well, but she certainly admired you. So do I. Come on. We must go to bed. I have plans for us to go sailing in the morning."

Emily got up off his knee with some reluctance. Then she regained her sense of humour. She gave him a cheeky grin. "The bikini looks pretty skimpy so you will see most of your present! Goodnight Simon. Thank you for being so honest and I really will enjoy any help you can give me."

Emily had wanted him so badly, but she realised it was not going to happen. However maybe it was for the best. She could not see how it was, but at least he had promised to help her. She consoled herself that men don't give bikinis to girls they don't find attractive. What a day. She stepped out of her dress, took off her underwear, wrapped her new kikoi around her, went to the bathroom and was soon asleep.

She woke when Simon brought her a cup of tea. She stretched and laughed,

"I will give you a job when Abdi takes some leave."

"I will take you up on that. It is a public holiday so I have given Jonathan the day off. I thought we could go straight down to the Yacht Club. They are racing today, but we could have a quick sail before they start. Then we could have breakfast there. It is always good. May I stay with you at Galana, when I fly you back and I will fly back in the very early morning like I did before?"

"Of course you can. I would love that." She got out of bed with her kikoi on, saying,

"See I'm wearing it already."

They were soon ready to go, after Simon had shouted to her that he had got towels. On the way he asked her if she had done any dingy sailing. Emily was pleased that she had done quite a lot in the UK with her brother. However Simon frightened her, when he said they would be sailing Five 0 Fives. Emily said he would have to help her with the trapeze.

Simon signed her in at the club. She whispered to him,

"Can I have one of the towels. I have got the new bikini on. It is really tiny. I will feel shy walking down from the changing rooms. Mercifully most of the members seem to have been celebrating late last night." Simon laughed,

"Of course you can. You can leave the towel on the beach." He handed her a bright beach towel. He waited for her to change. He thought how sensible she was wearing a shirt and her trainers which he told her were called 'tackies' in Kenya. He introduced her to Zachariah, the head boat boy. Simon helped her into the trapeze harness. She smiled at him and said,

"Did I give you permission to put your hand down there? I'm glad I have a harness on I feel virtually naked in this bikini. You are a very naughty boy. I love it."

Simon thought she looked gorgeous with her shirt unbuttoned with the ends tied under her breasts. She did not hesitate to jump into the water to help Zachariah launch the boat, calling to Simon to get in,

"You know what you are doing."

Emily found the rope for the trapeze and clipped herself on, so they were soon away. There was a good early morning wind and they raced across the harbour. Emily arched her back as far as she could on the trapeze. She knew that, as she was small, she had to use her weight to the best advantage. Simon just loved watching her. He realised what a beautiful figure she had. He imagined her under him arching her back like she was on the trapeze, to meet him. At that moment he regretted all his many dalliances. She was so young and so vibrant. He felt old and yet he was only seven years her senior. Their sail seemed so quickly over. They had to come in to let the racing crews get ready.

Emily thanked Zachariah and said that she worked a long way out into the bush, but hoped she would get a chance to come sailing again, as she had really enjoyed it. Zachariah was a giant of a man. Simon smiled to himself as he saw them together. She could have been a child. Emily saw him smiling and gave him quite a hard punch in his tummy,

"You old rogue. I'm trying my best at Swahili. It is your fault. You must teach me more."

She took off the harness and her soaking shirt. Simon could see that the bikini top was certainly a little small. She saw his look,

"Well, you now have virtually seen your present. Are you going to pack it up and send it back?"

Simon spluttered, "Certainly not. It is really beautiful. I did not realise that you had such.... He was going to say such great tits, but changed it to lovely breasts at the last minute."

The hesitation was not lost on Emily. She grabbed his hand as they walked up the beach. She reached up and whispered in his ear,

"You were sensible not to say anything rude, like my tits are a bit small. I gave you a gentle punch in the tummy a minute ago, but I'm at just the right height to give you a punch in the balls. Are they nice and big to give me a good target?"

Simon just shook his head and smiled. As they were looking at each other they had not seen Cynthia coming down the beach towards them. Emily looked up in horror, but controlled her features and said,

"Hi, Cynthia. I was just saying to Simon that he has got a lot of balls to take me sailing. I am hopeless. I hope you have a good race." She replied,

"I doubt it. I only win when Simon is at the helm." She walked on. Mike was carrying everything some way behind. When he met them he was friendly.

"Sorry about Cynthia, I think she has a bad head this morning!" Simon replied,

"Not a problem. Have a good sail."

When they got to the clubhouse, Emily asked if it would be OK for them to eat breakfast in their swimming things. Simon suggested that it might give him indigestion.

"Watch it Longfield, or do you enjoy having sore balls?"

He gave her a friendly smack on her bottom. She reached up and whispered,

"You had better be very careful. This bikini is so small and your hands are so large, any spanking marks will be visible and you will get a dreadful reputation!"

Simon had been right the breakfast was really good with lots of mangos and pawpaw for a start. Emily got juice down her chest, much to his enjoyment. She saw him looking and said,

"Am I going to get a spanking for my bad tables manners?"

"Not here, only when we get home."

"Promises, promises," was her reply

So with a lot of teasing it was a very enjoyable meal. They were left alone as everyone else was getting ready for the race. Simon signed the chit to pay and they left. Emily felt bad that she could not pay her share, but he told her she would be paying for all the meals he was going to have at Galana. Secretly this pleased her much more than anything else he could have said, as it suggested he intended to spend a lot of time up with her.

They stayed in their swimming costumes in the Landrover, as Simon said it would not hurt the seats. However just before Emily sat down he realised that the seat having been in the hot sun would burn her. He shot out his hand. Emily giggled,

"So you want to feel your present now, do you?" Simon stammered,

"I did not want you to burn your bottom on the hot seat."

Emily pushed her towel under her. As soon as they were going, she took his hand off the gear stick and put it on her thigh.

"Does your present feel alright?"

"Yes, nice and soft. It could be a bit browner just up here."

Emily had a line where she had been wearing shorts. She smiled at him. He moved his hand down her thigh. She took it and moved it back up saying,

"I will roll up the legs of my shorts when I'm working, but for now you will have to make do with the white strip. You have got fourteen days to return the goods you know!"

"I'll make do."

Emily felt a very lovely sensation as he gently stroked the skin of her inner thigh above the end of her tan. She could not stop herself from letting her legs fall apart as they went over a pot-hole. It was sadly too short a journey for both of them. Simon made a mental note, as he got out of the Landrover at his house that he must not touch so intimately. It was just not fair. He was sure he was going to make her sad. He must keep their relationship, as that of friends, not as lovers.

He packed up a small bag of things to take. He called through to her,

"You can leave any stuff here in your room it will be quite safe and save bringing clothes backwards and forwards." Emily's heart gave a leap. She called back,

"That would be great. The Galana Ball isn't for a few weeks, so I won't need my dress! However I am taking my presents. I can assure you I won't be wearing my hot old English pyjamas again in a hurry." Simon called back,

"You can leave them here. You might need them if we go somewhere cold upcountry for a weekend break. I will get Jonathan to wash them."

Emily thought, '*this is marvellous talking about weekend breaks. If I had my wish I would definitely forget my pyjamas. It seems as if my figure in the new bikini has been accepted. I will do some tanning in the new bikini to get rid of the tan marks.*'

When they went to get in the Landrover, Simon asked her if she wanted to drive. Emily jumped at the chance saying it would help her remember where she was going. Being a public holiday there was very little traffic on the causeway which ran off Mombasa Island. They were soon at the airport. Simon took her to the tower where he had to file his flight plan. He explained that the next morning he was allowed to file one in the air. He said he was going to be naughty in the morning and not get up as early, as he could switch radio frequencies and carry out the radio call to the stock route in the air.

Emily thought, *'If I had my way he would do the radio call in my bedroom!'*

Simon once again took her through all the procedures. He made her hold the stick and have her feet on the pedals, so she could feel what he was doing. Simon had already realised she loved flying. When they were properly airborne he encouraged her to fly the plane. She did not need any second bidding. He had got girls to fly planes before. They had always been hesitant and constantly looking at the instruments. Not Emily. She soon was climbing and descending, then turning off the heading they were meant to be on. She had a smile on her face the whole time. He explained that the plane they were in was called a Piper Colt. It was the most simple and cheapest to fly. It went very slowly and only had two seats. He said that he often flew a slightly bigger plane called a Piper Tripacer which had four seats and went a bit quicker. It was a high-winged plane and had a single front wheel, like the Colt. Emily turned to him and said,

"I've decided that I'm going to learnt to fly. I expect I will need an instructor, but will you help me to arrange it?" Simon's jaw dropped open. There was so much more to this young lady than he had imagined, when her sad little voice had come over the radio the morning after her Aunt had died.

As they walked on to the veranda carrying their light bags, Abdi came onto the other end with some coffee and cake. Simon said in Swahili,

"I think we smelt your cake in the aeroplane?" Abdi replied in Swahili,

"I'm sure Memsahib Mary would want you to come for my cake." Slightly hesitantly Emily said in Swahili,

"I think she would Abdi, you make the best cakes in Africa." His face broke into a smile. Emily added,

"Do you think we can give the Bwana a little light food for lunch and some supper?" Abdi replied,

"Certainly we can Memsahib."

When he had left, Simon laughed,

"You are certainly doing your best with your Swahili." She replied,

"It is probably the best way to learn. I can't communicate with the staff otherwise."

Over coffee they talked about her learning to fly. Simon told her she would have to come to Mombasa for a medical. Emily said that she did not really fancy Richard examining her. She would be too embarrassed. Simon said she did not have to worry, as only Ian was licensed to carry out flying medicals. He teased her and said she did not have to take her clothes off. He said he would try and fix it to coincide with a trip that he needed to take to Voi very soon. Simon said he would get all the forms she would need to fill in. He said he knew the two assistant flying instructors. He would ask them if they would take her on. He would ask Ken Gibb first, as he was a more relaxed guy and would be able to accommodate her easier, as she would have difficulty arranging the lessons from so far away.

They stopped talking about flying and Emily took Simon out to the farm office to show him what she had done with the cattle records and the veterinary cupboard. While they were there Colin Roberts arrived. He should have arrived back on the previous evening, but his Landrover had broken down at 'Hunters Lodge'. He had managed to get it fixed and so he had continued on. He had parked it on the South Bank of the river, where he normally kept it. He had waded across. Simon introduced him to Emily. He had known she was coming. He had heard some days ago about Auntie Mary's death. Simon thought he might have made some effort to get back sooner, but Simon said nothing.

Emily once again surprised him. She said how sad she was about Auntie Mary's death, but that she was determined that the ranch would carry on as Auntie Mary would have wished. Emily told Colin that he would receive a legacy, when the probate had been granted. Emily was very straight with Colin. She said she would be delighted if he would stay on and continue as he had before. However Emily said she would quite understand if he did not want to work for her, as she was an inexperienced young girl. If so she would totally understand if he left. She stressed that the ranch would continue to operate to some extent on the same lines, but that she would be bound to alter things, as she was likely to have new ideas particularly regarding the veterinary aspects. Emily asked him what time he started in the morning. He said he normally started at seven and

34

finished at two. Emily said that would be fine and that she would see him in the morning and they would make plans then. She said he must be tired and so he probably wanted to get back to his house and settle in after his holiday. Simon was amazed that Emily was so firm with Colin and congratulated her, when he had left. She smiled at him,

"I thought I had got to be straight with Colin. I wanted to make him understand that I was in charge. It's what I learnt dealing with old farmers, when seeing practice." She reached out and squeezed his hand. "I will have masses of time with Colin. I wanted to enjoy our evening alone together. We will not have many suppers together, as you will be working hard." Then she added with a cheeky grin, "You also have all these ladies to service in Mombasa!" Simon blushed and said,

"I think this leopard is going to change his spots!" Emily replied,

"I hope it does, but you have been very honest with me Simon. I want us to be good friends. Come on let's go back to the house and have lunch."

Over lunch they continued talking about flying. Suddenly Emily asked,

"Do you have to be a pilot to own a plane?"

"Certainly not."

"Why don't I get the ranch to buy one? I could then learn to fly quickly using it. I could run the ranch so much more efficiently with one. What sort of money would I need to get a Tripacer? Initially I would keep it at the aero club at Mombasa and then I could keep it up here. What do you think, Simon? I know you will be honest."

Simon looked at her with some surprise. They kept eye contact,

"I think that is a great idea."

The rest of the day was great fun. After lunch they drove to check up on one of the further away cattle bomas before having a walk along the river. They had a good supper and both went to bed laughing as they both called at the same time, "Sleep well!"

Chapter 4

The Christmas Holiday is Over

Monday 2nd January 1967

In fact they did sleep well. After breakfast, Emily came to the airstrip to wave him off. She was not sad. She had too much to do on the ranch. She did not stop to listen to Simon on the radio, but went straight to the office to get to work and be ready for Colin's arrival. He was half an hour late. Emily thought he looked tired, but also she could see he was hung over. She immediately wondered if he was an alcoholic. She kept her thoughts to herself. She had not said anything to Simon, but she had picked up on the fact that Simon was cross that Colin had not made any effort to get back to the ranch or contact her. She smiled to herself. Her love for Simon was not blind. She was getting to read him rather well. She knew in her heart that she wanted him to be her man, but she wanted it to be either a close friendship or a relationship of equals. She was amazed at herself that she had offered him her body and yet had not been heartbroken that he hadn't accepted it. She did not want to be in a line of past conquests, she wanted him to take her as his woman.

Her thoughts came back to the ranch. She got to work.

She started on the cattle records. She got her head around all the various mobs and where their bomas were at the moment. She realised that she would have to identify each animal. She knew that hot branding each animal was carried out elsewhere, but she thought that was barbaric and knew it was soon going to be illegal in the UK. Obviously Auntie Mary had not decided what to do. Emily had found a set of hot brands in the store, but they did not look as they had been used recently. Certainly none of the cattle had numbers branded on them. All they had was the Z brand which Simon had told her, was the Rinderpest Vaccination Brand. Most of the cattle were Boran cattle. They were *Bos indicus* with big humps and dewlaps. They were white in colour, but their skin under the hair was black, so freeze branding would not work. They had black colour in their ears, so tattooing would not work. Emily remembered her father talking about ear notching pigs to identify them. Perhaps that's what she would have to do. She knew that metal or plastic ear tags would get torn out by the thorns.

Abdi came down with a cup of coffee and a piece of cake. He had also brought the same for Colin. Emily took hers into Colin's office to be sociable. He did not seem that pleased to see her and did not bother to get up. She asked him how she could get the new spray race nozzles which they required. With rather bad grace he said he would order them from Nairobi. She talked to him about identifying the cattle. He was very negative and said he did not think it was necessary. Emily very wisely dropped the subject. She had been right. This was going to be a difficult relationship. His gratitude to Auntie Mary obviously did not extend to her niece. Emily wondered what happened at lunch. She was not looking forward to spending an hour with Colin. Then she relaxed. He had said he worked from seven until two, so it was likely that he went home then and had lunch at home.

She made a list of all the veterinary items of equipment which she would need. She would ask Simon first and if he thought it was appropriate she would get Colin to order them from Nairobi. Looking through the ledgers she had found that the ranch had an account with a chemist in Mombasa. She made a list of medicines she would need. She planned to pick them up from Mombasa, when she went for her medical. She knew Simon had registered her with the Kenyan Veterinary Board. This was only a formality as her degree allowed her to practice in Kenya. She just had to pay £5. She had given Simon a cheque to make it official, although he had tried to pay for her, however she wouldn't let him.

Julius came in to see her and asked if she would look at a sick new born calf at one of the nearer bomas. She was delighted. She had real veterinary work to do. She had made a bag before the holiday with some very basic equipment which she had found. So collecting it, she went in the Landrover with Julius. The calf was not ill as such, but had a very thick navel. She tied a tight nylon ligature around it and then sprayed it with gentian violet spray. She gave it an injection of penicillin. It was a bull calf. She asked Julius about the castration policy. He said he castrated all the bull calves which were not going to be kept for stock bulls, when they were weaned. Emily had read that late castration like this, caused a real check in their growth rates. She decided to change the policy and castrate the calves within the first 24 hours of birth with a rubber ring called an elastrator ring. She had found the applicator in the medicine cupboard. It was brand new. It was shiny and bright and still in its polythene bag. She showed Julius how to use it. She stressed to him how it was very important that the ring was placed above BOTH testicles or the calf would be a rig and still be fertile. Julius said he would be happy to do these castrations, but he said that he would like her to supervise him for the first few.

They discussed how each of the breeding bomas would have to have an applicator with some rings. He said the headmen would do the job if Emily would teach them. Emily smiled to herself. She was making herself useful at last. She imagined herself helping the enormous Turkana headmen to do the job. They were all eighteen inches taller that her! However she never felt intimidated by them. She always treated them with respect and they always seemed to show the same respect for her. Auntie Mary had advised her on their short time together that it was vital that she instructed the headman what she wanted done. He would then instruct the herdsmen. There was a rigid chain of command. Emily made a mental note to write down their names by the big boma chart in her office. She asked if they would mind if she took their photo to help her remember their names. Julius told her he did not think they would mind if she asked them, as none of them were Masai. They were all Turkana. Emily asked if they would like a copy of their photo to keep. Julius thought they would be delighted.

It was after two when they got back to the office. Emily was relieved that Colin had already left. She thanked Julius for his help and walked up to her house. She was really hungry. Abdi had a beautiful chicken curry ready for her. She attacked it with gusto.

After lunch she sat and had a coffee. She read one of the textbooks which she had bought on tropical diseases. She made some notes to ask Simon what she needed to be vaccinating against. In the afternoon she took one of the ranch Landrovers which she knew was the one that Auntie Mary drove. She checked the tool box under the seat. There were no tools to change a wheel and yet there was a spare which looked in good order and was pumped up, on the bonnet. She found the jack and the wheel brace in the workshop. She also selected a length of pipe to give her more purchase with the wheel-brace, as she was sure she would not be able to shift the nuts without it. She made sure that she had plenty of fuel and water in a couple of jerry cans. She took a big heavy torch which she had found in the office and set off. She had only gone fifty yards and she remembered the radio. She turned around and collected it. She thought that she would not need it and in fact it would not be much good as no one would be listening, but Simon had told her to take it. It was in a wooden padded box, so it was already to take on safari. The aerial and the battery were in separate boxes. Emily smiled. She would tease Simon. She would have to climb a tree to put the aerial up!

She followed the road which she had gone on before with Julius. She knew she was going in the right direction, as she could see the hill Daka Watchu on the sky line. She knew the boma containing calving cows was at the foot of the hill. She got to the boma in 45 minutes. She got out of the Landrover and watched the herd plodding into the boma, being led by a young Turkana who saluted her. It seemed strange that they were her cows. At the back was the headman. When he saw the Landrover he ran to her. He spoke in very guttural Swahili. Emily gathered that there was a sick cow at the back. He led her to the cow. Another herdsman was carrying her new born calf. The cow was not sick. It had prolapsed its uterus. Emily's heart sank. She had never had to deal with one before. However she knew what to do. She knew her attire would not have pleased the Professor of Surgery. She had on a short sleeved blue shirt, denim shorts and tackies. She asked the headman for some clean water and soap. She was glad she remembered her Swahili. The cow was held for her without a halter. There seemed to be masses of large tall men about, wearing very little. She felt very small, but not at all threatened. Her bag had been brought. She knew she had local anaesthetic and mercifully a clean syringe and the right size needle in a small steriliser tray. She gave the cow an epidural. It did not move a muscle. She also gave it some penicillin. Then using sign language she managed to get the headman to get the cow first on to the ground on its side and then on to its brisket. She thought then how lucky she was to have all these big strong men. She knew on English farms the vet was lucky to have an old farmer and a boy!

The men just watched her and when she actually put their hands on the cow's legs they were very gentle. She got the headman to have the cows back legs pulled out directly behind it. She then got the headman to sit on the cow facing its tail which she wanted held up like a flag. He obviously had never seen anything like this, but he smiled at her. Then she knelt between the cows back legs and rested the uterus on her thighs. She asked the headman to ask someone to bring the water near to her and wash the uterus, as she held it out of the dust. She was relieved that the after birth had been shed somewhere and was not attached to the uterus.

She thought, *'This organ is enormous. It will never go back!'* She was amazed that it was a bit of a struggle at first, but then it slipped in quite easily. She then asked for a glass bottle which was brought. She used this to extend her reach so she could push the uterus back completely. The headman realised what she was trying to do. He instructed another big man to sit on the cow and he knelt beside her. He let her wash his arm and then really gently he pushed the bottle into the cow. Emily thought his arm was nearly twice as long as hers. She wished she had a Seton needle and some uterine tape to put a stitch in the vulva. As she was getting up she looked up at the man holding the tail, so that she could tell him he could stop holding the tail. He had no shorts on, unlike the headman. She couldn't help noticing his enormous penis. She was going to have a laugh with Simon about this escapade. She looked down at herself. She was covered in blood and slime. She made a rather futile attempt to clean herself up. The headman indicated that she should wait. More water was brought. The headman suggested she put her arms above her head. Emily wondered what he was going to do. Was he going to wash her? He threw the big cooking pot of water at her. It was not cold but it made her catch her breath. She laughed and he smiled. Emily thought, 'I will have to be careful or he will claim me as his third wife.' However she instinctively knew he meant her no harm. To Emily's delight the calf was up and suckling. In the UK she would have given the cow an injection to close the uterus down. It was the same hormone which caused the cow to let her milk down, so she knew that nature had taken over. She asked the headman his name. He said he was called Kikapoi. She shook him by the hand. He brought his other enormous hand round and gripped her fore-arm and bowed his head. She knew she had gained his respect.

She drove back to the ranch with a happy heart. She just wished she could share her achievement with someone. Air letters apparently took forever even from Mombasa. She had not received anything from home. Obviously there was no telephone. The radio was her life line, but she didn't want to burden Simon too much. What she really wanted was a girlie chat. Then she laughed. She was better off here in this marvellous place, than having a girlie chat with Cynthia or Eve! They may be a good lay for Simon, but she was sure they could not replace a cow's uterus! She swung into Galana as the tropical night was failing fast. The hurricane lamps were lit and there was Abdi. She was sure of a good supper. She was also sure that the water would be hot for a lovely shower.

Abdi brought tea on to the veranda. He saw her messy state and smiled and said in Swahili,

"The Memsahib has been working hard. Johno the dhobi wallah will be happy doing the washing in the morning."

Emily took her tea into her room. She felt sexy as she stripped naked. May be she was also a good lay, as well as a good cattle vet. The hot shower was heaven. The evening breeze was lovely as it cooled her. So often she came out of the shower, even after a cold one, and immediately broke into a sweat. She ate her supper in her new kikoi.

She casually looked at her watch, as she went to get a book from her bedside table. It was exactly eight o'clock. She knew she was being foolish, but she connected the two leads from the radio to the battery and switched it on. It fired up and she pressed the microphone switch twice. She nearly jumped out of her kikoi as a voice said,

"Galana, this is PVO Coast do you read over?" She was so excited she nearly blurted out,

"Simon, my darling, is it really you?" Instead in a very controlled voice she said,

41

"PVO Coast this is a very surprised Galana. In fact so surprised she has dropped her present."

She let her kikoi fall and sat naked in front of the radio.

"Galana this is a very happy PVO Coast with a vivid imagination."

Emily felt an enormous blush spreading rapidly up her neck and face from her breasts. She managed to get herself back in control.

"I managed to replace a cow's uterus this afternoon. Cow and calf seem to be doing well, but I would have liked to have given her oxytocin (the hormone to reduce the size of the uterus) and have put in a stitch." She realised she had forgotten the proper procedure. However she did not think Simon minded as he just replied,

"You have done very well. You are a star. I have a pencil and paper handy. Do you want to give me a list of instruments and medicines which you need? I will get them for you. Your pilot's medical is provisionally arranged for the day after tomorrow. Obviously I won't have all of the medicines, but I will have some by then."

"I will drive down tomorrow. I will enjoy that as I will get to see some of the country."

"Arrive whenever you like. Jonathan will have supper ready whenever. We won't chatter now. It will be good to catch up, when I see you. Wrap up. PVO out."

Emily pressed the microphone switch several times. She meant them as kisses, but she didn't think he would realise. She was delighted that he knew she was naked. She wrapped herself in her kikoi and went and tried to read her book on the veranda. She still felt very hot and it was difficult to concentrate, but after a few minutes in the breeze she calmed down.

At breakfast she asked Abdi to pack up some lunch for her. Colin was late again. She said nothing, but just made a little mark in her diary. She told him where she was going and the reason. She asked him if he needed any stores from Mombasa. He said that would be helpful. He said he would make a list. As it was he made two lists, one for the ranch and one for him. She noticed there was six bottles of whiskey on his list. She was now certain he was an alcoholic. Julius insisted she took two members of staff with her; a young boy to guard the vehicle and a clerk called Alex, who would help to do the shopping. He always had done the shopping for Auntie Mary.

They left after coffee. There had not been any rain for some time, so in fact the road was not too bad. Eventually they came to a T junction on a big road. She knew she had to turn right to go south. Soon she was on Tarmac. This continued to a big steel bridge across the Sabaki. Emily smiled. It was really her river! She filled up in Malindi, but did not stop except for a coke. She bought one each for Alex and the young lad whose name was Tuku. He was particularly pleased. South of Malindi the Tarmac ended, but the murram road was good. In forty miles they came to Kilifi. Here she had to drive on to a ferry. She bought some cashew nuts. From then on they were on Tarmac. In thirty miles they came to another steel bridge at Mtwapa, where they had to pay a toll. It was fortunate that Emily had taken some money out of the petty cash in the safe. On this stretch she saw acres and acres of sisal. She also saw some big cows which were like hers, but were fawn in colour. She guessed they were Sahiwals, a breed she had read about from Pakistan. South of the bridge she saw some Jersey cows. In ten miles she reached a pontoon bridge at Nyali and had to pay again. She dropped off Alex and Tuku in Mombasa near to the one and only supermarket. She arranged to meet them there at coffee time on the following day as she knew the doctor's surgery was next door. Alex gave her directions to the Chini Club as he said Memsahib Mary always stayed there. It was easy for her to find her way to Simon's house.

As she drew up outside, Simon saw her from the upstairs veranda. He jumped up, waved both arms and shouted,

"Well done getting here. I was worried you would have a dreadful journey. I turned the radio on in case you had a problem."

They met on the stairs and much to Emily's joy they hugged. As they broke apart she teased him,

"You obviously think I am a Tom boy. How am I going to climb a thorn tree to get the aerial up?"

"Surely you have someone with you?"

"I have on this trip but I don't, when I am on the ranch"

"May be you should?"

"OK worry guts. I will think about it"

Emily was so delighted that he seemed so pleased to see her. Jonathan came rapidly upstairs with tea. He also seemed pleased to see her. He was soon up again with her bag. She joked with him saying in Swahili that she hadn't got any sewing jobs for him to do. He beamed with pleasure.

Emily was also pleased with the medicines that Simon had bought for her. She thanked him and made sure that he had put them on the ranch's account at the Chemist. Simon promised he had. He said he also had told the Chemist that she was a vet and therefore she would not have any problems sending any of her staff to collect medicines, in future. He had not got many of the instruments yet. However he had brought from the veterinary office some stuff which she was very welcome to borrow until hers arrived. This included a Seton needle for stitching a cow's vulva after a prolapse. Emily said she was rather glad she did not have one two days before, as the very thought of the stitch made her squirm. Simon laughed,

"You will regret not stitching when it all comes back out again in a few hours." Emily said,

"I got an enormous Turkana chap to put his arm in with a bottle. I don't think it will come out again."

She giggled when she told Simon about the chap without any shorts! She also made him laugh about having water thrown over her. Simon did not say anything because he did not want to sound patronising, but he was very proud of her. He could not think of any other girl who would have done what she did, on her own. Also he knew that she would do it again without any hesitation.

Simon apologised that he hadn't fixed up a dinner party. Emily was delighted, as she enjoyed it much more with just the two of them.

It was over supper that Simon told her his really big news. He had found a good Tripacer for sale. It belonged to a German man who lived in Moshi, in Tanzania near to Kilimanjaro. Simon said he was happy to fly her up, if they combined it with a visit to Betty and Jack at Voi. However he said she must get through her medical tomorrow first. Emily said she thought she would be OK. She knew her heart was OK and colour blindness was extremely rare in girls. She had had a compulsory medical only four years ago when she went to

Bristol. She did not have diabetes and there was no history of epilepsy in her family. Simon said,

"Are you sure you don't want me to sound your heart out. I have brought a stethoscope from the surgery." She stuck her tongue out at him saying,

"Dream on Longfield." She actually thought her heart would race uncontrollably with his hand anywhere near her chest.

Simon got her filling in all the forms for her to get her provisional Private Pilots License (PPL) He also said that unlike in the UK she had to have a radio-telephonist's license. She had to fill in more forms. He gave her all the books he had used to get his written exam, together with the special square protractor which pilots had to use for navigation.

The evening was such fun. It was nearly midnight when they turned in. She had been put in the same room which she had used before. Jonathan had laid out her hot old pyjamas. She put them in the chest of draws and slept in the nude but with her kikoi handy in case he brought tea in, in the morning.

They hugged as Simon said goodbye and left for the veterinary office. Emily loaded up the Landrover with the kit that Simon had acquired for her. He had also lent her a couple of text books and another book on learning Swahili. Jonathan shook her hand with a smile and said she was welcome anytime in this house. He said he was sure Bwana Simon would be happy for her to come to stay even if he was away on safari.

The medical went well and Emily passed with flying colours. Alex and Tuku were waiting by the Landrover as planned. They set off without delay. Mercifully their journey went well. Colin had been at work, but he had left before they arrived back at the ranch. However Julius reported that all was well at all the bomas. Emily thought she was getting like an old mother hen wanting to get back to her nest and to know all was OK. That night when she flicked the radio on there were three distinct clicks of a microphone switch. Emily replied with three clicks of her own. Were the first, three kisses from Simon? She wanted to think so!

Emily was up promptly in the morning. She had done some serious thinking about what to do about Colin. This state of affairs could not continue. She had decided to give him a project to see if he could focus on one task. He was half an hour late yet again. Her calendar showed her that in fact he had not been on time any morning. After Julius had given her his report about the cattle she asked him to go down to Mr. Colin's office and ask Mr. Colin to come up to see her at 9 o'clock. This gave her time to do some of the tasks on her list and collect her thoughts before the meeting. She also thought it was less confrontational than calling him up immediately.

He did arrive on time, but he did not look well. Once he had shut the door she asked him to sit down. She did not mince her words. She said she was aware that he had a drinking problem and asked whether there was anything she could do to help. She was amazed when he broke down in tears, saying,

"Is it that obvious? My niece did not notice over Christmas." Emily got up and put her arm around him and said,

"It is probably this remote place that is making everything worse. Do you feel lonely here?" He sobbed,

"Yes. When I heard that Mary had died I knew I should return, but I just could not face it. I only came back because my niece would have thought it was odd if I hadn't. I told my niece that you would have everything under control. I did not know you were only a young girl. I feel so guilty now."

Emily needed more information, so that she could help him and asked,

"I know it is none of my business, but how are you managing financially?" Colin drew in a breath and said,

"My problem is here in Kenya. My ranch failed and Mary helped me. She was a very strong woman and a good friend to me. She gave me this job, but under certain conditions. I was not to drink again and I was to leave my assets which I had in the UK, in the UK. She said she would say to everyone that it was the drought which made my ranch fail. This helped as I didn't feel such a failure." She drew up a chair so she could sit next to him. He was not a big man and so she could put her arm around him. She switched tack and asked,

"Have you any family in England?"

"Yes, I have an unmarried sister, also called Mary. She has often asked me to come and live with her. We own her house jointly, as it was left to us by our mother. There is money in a trust for the two of us in the UK." Emily asked,

"Would you like to return to the UK?"

"Yes, I would."

"Would you like me to help you to return to the UK?"

He started to cry again,

"I can't because I can't get income tax clearance." Emily had heard that caused problems. At some stage she was going to have to sort out her own life. She was only here on a visitor's visa, as Auntie Mary had bought and open return airfare. She didn't want to trouble Colin with her problems and said,

"How much tax do you owe?"

"I owe over £2000 sterling. I have only four hundred shillings in my account. I know, as I drew out the money for the groceries you brought up from Mombasa for me."

"I will get the solicitors in Mombasa to pay your tax bill with an advance from your legacy of £5000 from Auntie Mary. I will also get the solicitors to buy you a ticket to the UK. Would you like to go by sea or by air?"

He did not reply immediately, but for the very first time he looked her in the eye and then said,

"Mary made a good decision when she invited you out here. You have her blood running in your veins. What is your advice?" Emily did not hesitate,

"I would advise you to go by sea. Hopefully when you are not lonely and stressed you may be able to stop drinking. It will take strength. You have that strength. I'm sure you don't want to let Auntie Mary down." He actually smiled then,

"Very well I will go by sea." Emily then made a very kind, but difficult decision.

"In the mean time you will move in with me here. You will continue to draw your salary and we will work out what you are due for leave pay. This will give you money on the boat and when you first get to The UK. You will be able to take your belongings with you on the boat. I am a hard taskmaster. I want you to build a causeway across the Galana. I am going to call it 'Colin's Causeway'. I'm going to have a stone sign put beside it to remind us of you. Will you do that for me and Auntie Mary?" Colin could see tears in her eyes now. He replied,

"I would be honoured to do it. Thank you Emily, for giving me this chance. I will do my best not to let you down."

He moved in with her that day. They had lunch together. Then he went and got the stuff he needed for now from his house and brought it to Galana. Emily moved into Auntie Mary's room and he moved in to her room. She smiled to herself. If Simon comes to stay he will have to share a room with me! Colin was concerned about his old cook. Emily said she would take him on the payroll of Galana. She said he could maintain Colin's house. She would make some improvements to it and then rent it out as a lodge to bring in extra revenue. She said she would buy any furniture which he did not want. She also would buy his Landrover.

Colin set to work on making the causeway with a passion. He got up at the same time as her. Abdi made him a good breakfast and all his other meals. The whiskey sat on the side board. Neither of them had a drink. Colin set a gang of men improving the fire-break road up from the Tarmac at Mackinnon Road. Most days Christmas drove the lorry to get supplies from Mombasa. This was mainly cement from Bamburi Cement Company. Emily often sent Alex with Christmas with letters to the solicitors and other instructions. Rather than have a long conversation on the radio she sent a letter to Simon telling him what was happening. She also asked him to recruit a clerk to take over Colin's clerical duties. When Colin's passage was booked, Emily and Simon arranged a memorial service for Auntie Mary which could also be Colin's farewell party.

Emily talked very frankly with Colin one night.

"Would you be OK, with having to keep off alcohol at a lunch time do, at Mombasa Club?" She was saddened and quite touched when he replied,

"Yes if you are there with me."

Chapter 5

Auntie Mary's Memorial Service

Wednesday 18th January 1967

Emily was amazed how full Mombasa Cathedral was. Simon had been right. Auntie Mary had obviously been well liked and respected. There was no parading down the aisle. Emily sat at the front flanked by Colin and Simon. She had organised for Christmas to bring the lorry down with any staff who wanted to come. Obviously many of the herdsmen hardily knew her and they were happy to stay and guard the cattle as normal. It was mainly the office and house staff who came. Emily read one of the lessons and Colin read the other. Mercifully the bishop gave a very short address. Emily was surprised to see so many Europeans. Many she remembered from the New Year's Eve dance. However there was a large number of upcountry ranchers who Simon said had flown down. He said Mombasa airport probably looked like Piccadilly Circus. As they came out of the cathedral Emily saw Kikapoi with several of the herders from that Boma. Somehow they had managed to get long trousers, some of which were on the short side. She was relieved they had their blankets, but not their spears. She went up and greeted them. Simon was a little alarmed as they all crowded around her and as she was so short he could not see her. However he knew all was well as there was a lot of laughter. Simon had organised for all the staff to have a party at the veterinary office. His PA, a lovely old man called Silas was in charge with Julius. The staff went with Christmas followed by Emily and Colin in a Landrover. Simon had been left with Ian to host the lunch at the Chini club. Emily and Colin did not spend long at the Veterinary Office. They both gave a small speech and that was it except, unexpectedly Kikapoi gave them a big cheer which all the staff joined.

When they got to the Chini Club, the party was well under way. Emily was glad she was now a member and so the secretary was very helpful. There was plenty of drink and small canapés.

Simon was just talking to Emily saying how he was slightly apprehensive when she was surrounded by so many tall Turkana herdsmen, when Cynthia came over to them. She obviously wanted to talk to Simon, but had to put up with talking to them both.

"I've just been talking to Colin. I gather he sails back to the UK later today as he is retiring. However will you manage out in the wilds, when you are all alone? I gather it is a four hour drive and you have to wade through a crocodile infested river to get to your home." Emily laughed,

"Thanks to Colin's Causeway there is no more real wading to do unless there has been a lot of rain upriver. Colin has also improved the firebreak road so it now only takes two and a half hours. Why don't you and Mike come up one weekend? I am in the process of improving Colin's house and making it in to a lodge. It has a wonderful view of the river and we have a mass of game."

Mike had joined the group,

"That sounds a splendid idea. I would love to see your cattle. I'm sure we could come to a deal for me to buy your steers on a regular basis. It might suit both of us. It costs me a fortune to rail big steers down from upcountry."

Cynthia did not look as if she liked that idea at all. Emily thought, however, that she might jump at the idea if Simon was coming. They were then joined by a very good looking fair-haired man in his thirties who introduced himself as Jack Short. He said he had a ranch at Ulu which Emily remembered passing on her first journey down from Nairobi. It seemed so long ago. He said to her,

"So you are a rancher. You must come up to my place and see how ranching should be done." Emily replied.

"I'd like that." She actually thought you may be a good looking guy, but I think you are very arrogant, so she added,

"Give me a few years and maybe you can come to Galana and see how we ranch in the hot country!"

"Water must be your big problem."

"Yes you are right, it is so important for us to get the cattle a good way from the river. Then supervision is a problem. I long to be able to get my PPL, so that I can fly." He replied,

"Oh, that's an overrated pastime." Emily thought she was getting a little sick of this chap so she turned and introduced Mike and Cynthia to him. Emily was delighted as Cynthia's body language changed. She thought maybe you are right for each other. She moved away and smiled as her body language must have told Simon something, as he moved with her. She whispered in his ear,

"He is seriously arrogant. The next thing will be that he will be telling me that I'm too small to calve down cows!" Simon whispered back,

"I have not met him before, but I heard he tried to learn to fly, but could never manage to go solo. Somehow he could not judge distances."

Emily sniggered, but then said very seriously,

"I hope that doesn't happen to me!" Simon reassured her,

"It won't. I'm sure you are going to be a natural."

Simon and Emily went with Colin to the boat. As she kissed him goodbye she whispered,

"Remember whenever you think you would like a drink, think of me. You will then think, thank goodness I haven't got that nagging old witch living with me!" He had tears in his eyes when he replied,

"I would follow you to the ends of the earth." She answered,

"What a lot of poppycock. Anyway Galana is the end of the earth. You have a good time on the boat. I want lots of letters and lots of gossip. I have your sister's address so I will bore you with all the happenings at Galana, and I will be seeking your advice. Every time I have a swim, I will think of you."

Colin laughed then,

"I will never forget you jumping out of your skin when you sat on that crab. I only wish your bikini had fallen off." She replied,

"You would not have seen much more, it was skimpy enough as it was!"

With that, she pushed him up the gang-plank.

As they walked away from the boat, Simon said to her,

"You are a marvel. You bring out the best in everyone. I think even Cynthia might come up to stay at Galana. Mike certainly would!"

She grabbed his hand saying,

"I think she would only come if you were there. I don't mind what you do in Mombasa, but I would make you behave at Galana." He answered,

"I promise you I am a changed man." Emily giggled,

"You might not get a look in, if Jack Short is around. That is provided he doesn't live up to his name!"

"Emily, you are impossible."

They had a good evening together. In the morning he went to work, she followed and blew her horn as he turned off to the Veterinary Office, as she was going for her first flying lesson.

Chapter 6

Emily Learns to Fly

Thursday 19th January 1967

They still had not managed to get up to see the Tripacer which was for sale, so Emily started to learn on the Colt, as she was so impatient. She liked Ken Gibb and she thought he was a good instructor. He amused her, as he was always either looking at her legs or down her top. However he never touched her or really invaded her space, so she didn't mind. It was too hot in Mombasa to wear trousers so she wore shorts. After a couple of lessons she said to him,

"You know I think you spend more time looking at my legs than at the instruments. We could be upside down for all you know." He gave her an innocent smile,

"I'm sorry but I think they are the most gorgeous legs I have ever seen?"

"You do talk a lot of rubbish. Now pay attention and tell me what I'm doing wrong."

He did then try harder. Emily had met his wife and their two children, when she had dropped him off at the aero club, when his wife had wanted the car. It had been arranged that Emily would drop him off after the lesson. His wife was a lovely cheerful girl, but Emily did notice she was rather Rubenesque.

Simon had been right, Emily was a natural flier. She loved it and had a good sense of balance and direction. She had only been flying with Ken for seven hours, most of which had been circuits and bumps, when he made her stop on the enormous runway. Mombasa took long haul jets. He got out of the plane saying,

"Just do a couple of circuits on your own and then taxi to the club house."

Emily broke out into a sweat, but then calmed herself and did two good landings. Sweat was running down between her breasts as she parked the plane. She met him in the coffee room,

"Look at me. I am in a muck sweat. You might have warned me that you were going to let me go solo."

"I usually don't as most trainees get flustered, if they think they are going to go solo. Then they make a botch of a landing and then I don't dare to let them go solo until they have had another lesson. Do you want to do another half hour of circuits?"

"Oh yes please."

"Go on then. I rang the tower. The Nairobi flight is not due for an hour."

Emily enjoyed her half an hour. The sweat had dried when she parked up for good.

She had two more lessons, one of which she was solo. Ken let her leave the circuit and do some local flying. Emily was ecstatic as she drove back to Galana. She longed to tell Simon. She got a chance the next morning as Simon asked her if she could be ready at 7.15 the following morning as he had to go to Jack and Betty's ranch. He did not need to say they were going on a swan to see the Tripacer at Moshi.

Jack had a hundred cows already in a coral when they arrived. Emily was delighted as Simon suggested they both did the pregnancy diagnosis, as there were two separate cattle races. Emily knew she had Simon as a backup if she was doubtful about a cow, but she did not have to use him, as they were all more than five months in calf. It was too hot to wear waterproof gowns so they had each worn old shirts and shorts. They got covered in dung. However Betty took them into the house so they could each have a shower. Simon, a little to Emily's sadness, was very proper and let her totally finish in the shower and bedroom before he came in. Betty wanted them to stop for lunch, but they declined as they wanted to get to Moshi.

Neither of them had remembered to bring their passports. Simon wondered if the authorities might be awkward, as officially he, as the pilot in charge, did not need one, but Emily, as she only had a provisional license did need one as Tanzania was a separate country.

However no one at the airfield even bothered to come and see them. Norbert Drager who was selling the Tripacer was there to meet them. He was very efficient and had all the paper work there, for them to see. The plane was blue and had been registered in Kenya before Norbert bought it, so it had a Kenyan call sign 5YHAT (5 Yankee Hotel Alpha Tango). Emily immediately called it Hattie, although when she was flying she would use the final two letters, alpha tango. Simon on her behalf had already agreed a price. He also had arranged insurance for him to fly Hattie.

Strictly speaking Emily should not have flown the aero club Colt, as she had not done a cross country with her instructor. However Ken Gibb had cleared it with Tom Dove the Chief instructor, as they were flying together and therefore Emily should not get lost. Emily had brought cash which she had got out of the ranch account in Mombasa, so without any ceremony they shook Norbert's hand, filed flight plans and after doing their aircraft checks took off. Emily was not really nervous as she was flying the Colt which she had done all her flying in, up to that time. She had decided she would have a couple of lessons with Ken in Hattie, as being a Tripacer it had some extra features. The main one was it had flaps to help landing and takeoff.

She took off first and after clearing the circuit set her heading for Mombasa. Simon took off after her and did the same. The Tripacer could go twenty knots faster than the Colt so he soon caught her up. He then throttled back and flew beside her, leaving her plenty of room. He was near enough to see her wave at him.

The flight was uneventful. Emily made a beautiful landing and taxied over to the aero club. Simon followed her. When they had both shut down their engines and got out, Emily just could not stop herself from wrapping her arms around him. She was so excited about owning an aeroplane. For once she did not feel him freeze.

They went home to supper as Jonathan was expecting them. Emily could tell even Simon was excited. However they were chaste as normal, when they went to bed. Once again in the morning they went in convoy with Simon turning in to the veterinary office and Emily going for a lesson with Ken. She had been feeling guilty that she had been away so much from Galana, so she asked Ken if he would fly up and give her a lesson on the Galana strip. She was sad that she wouldn't be seeing Simon.

In fact she did not see him for some time, as Ken, not only flew up for a couple of lessons, but also flew up so she could fly her first official cross country. Galana was so vast she could fly far enough without leaving the ranch.

She made use of this cross country to study the ranch from the air. She visited all the airstrips. There were vast tracks of country with no cattle. She knew that she had two major problems; Lack of water and Tsetse fly. Simon had told her that tick-borne disease was not a problem in the Northern part of the ranch. She remembered he wanted to make a new stock route down from the Tana River.

To get her PPL she, not only needed to take a flying test which she could do at Mombasa, but also she needed to take a written exam which she could also do at Mombasa. She had been studying the books which Simon had lent her. The written exam really did not seem difficult. Simon had given her the papers he had sat and some that he had been given by another candidate in the past. She thought they should not give her a lot of problems

Chapter 7

Emily Rescues Leonard

Tuesday 31st January 1967

In the morning she apologised on air for bothering him, but she asked him if he would fix up for her to sit her written exam. He said that was no bother. He said he was going to Mombasa Airport tomorrow. In fact if she was free would she like to come with him. He was going to visit Garsen, where there was a problem with LMD cattle crossing the river. Emily was never one to play hard to get. She said she would love to come. She said he was welcome to bring Hattie if it would be easier. She said she knew she could not log the hours as he wasn't an instructor. One of the conditions for getting her PPL was that she logged forty hours.

Simon said he would pick her up at 7.15. He also said a bikini and a pair of old tackies might be useful. Emily wondered what he had in mind.

She packed her very small bag after supper so she was all ready. She briefed Abdi and Julius that she would be away for the day. She said to Julius if there was a problem it was not vital she went, so she just would stay on Galana. Julius had grown fond of her and he knew she respected him. He smiled and said he thought he could manage!

Emily found it difficult to get to sleep as she was excited, so she was still asleep when Abdi brought in her tea. However she had plenty of time to dress, pop down to the ranch office and see Julius and eat her breakfast. She heard Simon coming and walked up with a lot of control to the airstrip. Simon did not stop the engine but swung Hattie round so it was easy for Emily to get in. Unlike the Colt, Hattie had two front doors and one rear door. Emily felt cheeky and kissed him on the cheek after she had shut her door, as he gunned the engine to taxi back up the airstrip. He shouted,

"Harness and Hatches." She replied,

"You are a rude bugger. Don't I get a Good Morning!" He squeezed her thigh,

"Sorry, Good Morning and thank you for my kiss and the loan of your airplane."

They were silent until he had taken off and set a heading for Garsen. It was only going to take them eighteen minutes. Emily shouted,

"I'm sorry to be grouchy. I look at life differently from you. I know we have to be just good friends, but I am in my own little world up here and you have a busy life at work and socially. I'm very pleased you invited me. Thank you." He gave her a big smile.

"Thank you for coming. It is because we are just good friends and because you are a veterinary colleague that I feel I can take you on government work. I don't take other visitors. Going to Jack and Betty was different as that was private work."

"I feel bad now. Did you have to take that as a day's leave?"

"I suppose I should have, but I didn't, as visiting big ranches can be considered as work." Emily could not stop herself giggling,

"So you don't have to take a day's leave to come and see me as a rancher, but you would do if you spent the day bouncing on top of me! Poor old Cynthia, if you take her down on to the South Coast for a day out and a shag, you have to take that as a day's leave which I know are precious, as you only get fourteen days local leave in your two year contract! Remember I applied to come out here on an ODA contract and they turned me down!"

Emily thought it was very funny that he had gone very red and stammered,

"Things are very different now."

Before she could say any more, he called on the radio,

"Alpha Tango inbound to Garsen from Galana reporting long finals two seven zero."

They were soon on the ground. Simon parked up, checked the magnetos and cut the engine. There was a Government Landrover driving towards them. Emily was surprised. It was not a Veterinary Department vehicle, but in big letters on the door was, 'District

Commissioner's Office'. Out got the most enormous man Emily had ever seen. He was a couple of inches taller that Kikapoi, but instead of being thin he was very well built. He could have been a heavy weight boxer. He was obviously a friend of Simon's as they embraced. Simon said,

"Leonard. I would like you to meet Emily Barrington-Long. She is a vet and is Mary's niece."

Emily put out her hand. She felt like a child meeting a very important person. He surprised her by putting his enormous hands on her shoulders and looking straight into her eyes.

"I was very sorry about her death. Also I was sorry not to attend her memorial service. I was summoned to Nairobi. I am going to be your next door neighbour, Simon." Simon beamed,

"Congratulations." Turning to Emily he said,

"That means that Leonard is now the Provincial Commissioner (PC) of the Coast Province." Leonard still had his hands on her shoulders and looked again into her eyes. She managed to say,

"Should I curtsey?" Leonard said,

"Certainly not. I thought it was ridiculous that my female contemporaries at Cambridge had to curtsey to your Queen. Mind you she seemed a nice woman. She was about your height." Emily could not resist saying,

"Did you put your hands on her shoulders?" Leonard laughed,

"Do you mind? I thought you looked so young and so beautiful." Emily went bright scarlet, but managed to say,

"Thank you for that compliment. I will treasure it for the rest of my life!" Leonard said,

"I also think you are very tough. I'm glad you are here because I think Simon and I will need some help here today. Come on we have work to do."

He turned to his Landrover and said to his driver in Swahili,

"Do you mind going in the back with the Askaris (Literally soldiers, but used to cover tribal police men), Jacob. I will drive and this young lady can sit next to me."

So Emily found herself squeezed in between Leonard and Simon. Behind her were ten khaki clad men with Rifles. She thought, '*Not long ago I was a humble little veterinary student, now I'm going to war to help the biggest man in Africa!*'

59

They drove into the village. There was a great throng of naked men who did not seem very pleased to see them. Leonard got out of the vehicle. He climbed on to the bonnet, although it was hardily necessary as he could easily be seen. Simon and Emily stood with the Askaris in front of the Landrover. He made a very short speech saying how for many years the government had paid the Pokoma men of this village one Kenyan shilling for every government cow which they have swum across the river. Why will they not continue with this arrangement?

A small man with very grey hair, replied that he and his men did not think this was enough for this dangerous job as there were more crocodiles and hippos in the river than before.

Leonard replied that he had brought Askaris to frighten off the crocodiles.

The old Chief replied that it was still very dangerous. Would the DC like to do the task?

Leonard replied that he would be happy to help not only the Provincial Veterinary Officer but also this young lady who needed the cattle for her ranch. He said confidently that the Government of Kenya would arrange to swim the Government's cattle across the river.

As he descended from the Landrover a lorry arrived on the other side of the river. Forty Turkana tribesmen got down from lorry. A Landrover also arrived which Emily could see had a rubber boat on top of it. There was a melee as the boat plus a small outboard motor were manhandled by veterinary staff into the river. Cattle had also arrived on the far bank of the river.

Leonard then said,

"We must get ready for our swim Simon. If you would like to stay in the Landrover my dear, my driver will look after you."

"Oh no Leonard, I'm also coming swimming." She started to unbutton her shirt. Leonard smiled,

"I was right you are tough!"

A long rope was being ferried across the river. Simon and Leonard had now got on their swimming trunks. Leonard looked even more imposing to Emily without his clothes. Her courage was beginning to fail her. The Tana River looked much wider and deeper than the Galana. Her bikini felt even smaller. However no one

60

worried about her nudity as most of the men were naked. Another lorry load of Turkana had arrived on the South bank of the river. Emily gave a start. There was Kikapoi. He was in charge. He came up to Emily. It was not Kikapoi, but a man extremely like him. Emily said in Swahili,

"You must be Kikapoi's brother." The man bowed, but Emily offered her hand which was gripped in the African manner with both hands. In very guttural Swahili, he replied,

"Yes." Then he put his hands around her biceps, as if he was going to apprehend her,

"My brother says you are great doctor. You must be very strong to treat cows. I salute you." With that he turned and started organising his men. They were obviously the collecting party this side of the river. Emily asked Simon what was now the plan. He said he hadn't realised that Leonard was going to help him, but he had been determined to cross the two thousand head of cattle destined for holding at a veterinary holding ground further South called Kurawa. They had started running out of grazing north of the river as the Pokoma had been so awkward. He said he could not pay them any more money as it had all been decided years ago by the Government.

Emily heard shouting from the far bank. The rope was across the river. The plan was for Simon and some of his men who could swim to line the rope. They would guide the cattle so that they did not get carried away by the current, by beating the water with sticks. Now they would be joined by Leonard and Emily. Emily could see that the herders planned to push the cattle into the water several hundred yards further upstream so they could get out of the water at this point, further downstream. She saw that there was a small ferry which could take a lorry across, but Simon said it was out of action at the moment and anyway they always swam the cattle across as it would take weeks to get them across in a lorry.

Emily noticed that Simon and Leonard worked well together, but that Simon normally deferred to Leonard. Simon had to make most of the small decisions. She saw them talking and then they quickly looked at her. She waved to indicate she would do whatever was required of her. However obviously the two men had agreed that Leonard would look after her. Simon was picked up by the rubber boat. Leonard called to her to follow him and he made his way into the water with a stick. An Askari gave her a stick and she followed Leonard into the water. It was the same temperature as the Galana and so actually it was quite warm, but it still made her gasp when it came above her bikini bottoms. It was not easy going along the rope hand over hand and still holding her stick but she managed. She was soon out of her depth. She could see Leonard was aiming for the middle of river. The current got much stronger and was relentlessly pushing her against the rope. She wondered how Leonard was managing considering his enormous bulk. She thought he must be immensely strong. She realised what force there was against her slim body.

There were other men coming from the other bank. They were strung out across the river with Leonard roughly in the middle. She was about ten yards from him. There were other men who had come behind her from the South bank. There was lots of shouting and the first cattle were urged into the water. They stepped cautiously into the deeper water and then did big leaps causing lots of splashing. Then they started to swim. They were good swimmers. They held their noses up with their necks stretched out. Their bodies were flat on the surface of the water and their tails stretched out behind them as they swam in what for a human was doggy paddle. They swam swiftly. Emily doubted if she would have been able to keep up with them even at her fastest crawl and she always thought of herself as a good swimmer.

She had one arm hooked over the rope and her back to it. She beat the water with her stick and shouted anything that came into her head. It reminded her of going beating in the woods on the farm in winter at home on shoot days. She shouted,

"Cock, cock, cock," as if they were pheasants. Then she giggled as she remembered the enormous naked Africans.

All proceeded as planned. She and Leonard kept shouting and laughing together. She had lost Simon and thought he must be on the North bank as the boat was still in the river patrolling between the cattle and the rope at the start until the cattle got the hang of the direction in which their friends had gone. At intervals the cattle which were obviously in mobs would stop being urged into the water and then herdsmen would be ferried across to help herd them away. It was during one of these lulls when the boat was full up with men that disaster struck. A large log came down the river half submerged. Initially Emily thought it was a crocodile and was speechless, but then she realised it was a log. It came straight at Leonard. Her shouted warning, came much too late. The log hit him on the head. He must have lost his hold on the rope as the next second he was being washed away downstream by the current.

Emily did not hesitate. She let go of her stick, ducked her head under the rope and swam after him. The current was taking them both at the same speed, but as she was swimming hard she soon caught him up. He must have been dazed as he was not swimming, but she was relieved that he was floating with his head above the water. She grabbed his arm and shouted for him to hold her shoulders. He held them in a vice like grip in a similar way to the way he had held her, when they had first met. In this manner Emily had the use of both her legs and arms. He was on his back as she swam with the current, but at an angle towards the South bank. He had blood streaming down his face. Soon Emily could feel the current lessening as she swam near to the bank. A water eddy helped her and then at last as she was weakening she felt the muddy bottom. Leonard said,

"Oh thank you, I can crawl now." Emily said,

"Wait it is still quite deep and muddy. I will swim and push you over the mud then you can crawl."

This she did and then as she was so tired she could not stand either, so when he had rolled over they both crawled through the mud together to get to the bank.

Where they were, was an oxbow of the river and the mud soon turned to sand. Emily could then get up and she helped Leonard to stand. She but her arm around his large waist and they struggled up under a tree together. She could see blood was still flowing from his eye. She got him to sit down and she knelt before him saying,

"You have a nasty cut. Let's have a good look at it?"

She could now see that he had a deep four inch cut below his left eyebrow which was still actually pumping blood. She was relieved that his eye looked OK. She had nothing else, so she took off her bikini top, made it into a pad and told him to hold it really tightly against his eye socket. She laughed with him saying,

"I would not feel safe with most men without my bikini top, but I feel safe with you." He replied,

"You risked your life for me. You never need be afraid of me. I will protect you and come to you whenever you need me."

These words might have had various meanings, but she took them at face value. However she just could not stop wondering what it would be like to make love to him. He was just so big!

Soon they heard the outboard motor and the boat came round the corner with Simon and one of the boatmen from the veterinary department on Lamu Island. Leonard shouted to them to be careful not to get stuck as the bottom was very muddy. The boatman cut the engine and lifted it out of the water. Simon jumped into the water with the painter and pulled the boat into the shallows. Leaving the painter with the boatman he ran up to them. He pretended not to notice Emily's lack of bikini top and concentrated on Leonard.

"What happened? The men suddenly noticed you missing."

Emily answered,

"Leonard was hit by a big submerged log. He has got a bad cut below his eyebrow which needs stitching. Mercifully his eye ball looks fine." Leonard added,

"It must have knocked me out. I was dazed, when I realised that Emily was holding on to me and keeping me up. I can see out of the eye. There is nothing wrong with my vision."

By the time they got back to the crossing point all the cattle were across. All that could be seen of them was the dust, as they made their way in mobs to Kurawa. The veterinary staff from there had already left to prepare for their arrival. The disgruntled Pokoma had disbursed.

Emily suddenly realised her nudity and scuttled to the Landrover. She found her shirt and quickly put it on. She found Simon's veterinary bag and guessed that he was going to stitch up Leonard's eye, so she brought the bag back to where he was sitting under a big tree. Simon had other ideas,

"You do the stitching, Emily. You will be much neater than me. I will go and sort out my people from Lamu so they can get back. They have done a wonderful job today, thanks to your leadership, Leonard." So he left them and went back to the river.

Emily got Leonard's driver to get out some clean water out of the Landrover. She cleaned the wound with some Iodine saying,

"I'm sorry this is going to sting."

She was pleased to see Simon had boiled syringes with fine needles and local anaesthetic which she carefully injected either side of the wound. Leonard did not move a muscle. Simon had a stitch up kit already sterilised. She got the driver to hold it for her. Then rather hesitantly she sat facing Leonard sitting on his knees as she could get to the wound better.

He smiled at her,

"You are so light you could be one of my children." She asked,

"How many children have you got?" He laughed,

"I'm a very modern African. I only have one wife and four children. At the moment where I am based at Galole there is no good school, so they all remain at Marsabit. However we are all pleased, as they will all be able to come down to Mombasa." Emily added,

"I've seen your house in Mombasa, you will have plenty of room."

As she was carefully placing the individual stitches, he told her about his time in the UK at Cambridge. He told her that he had learnt to swim when he started to row.

Emily thought, *'thank goodness he did not box. He would have killed his opponents.'*

They discussed what he was going to do about the Pokoma. Emily hesitantly suggested,

"If there is not a school here why don't you have one built before you leave the district to show your goodwill. I know you can't alter the amount of money they receive from crossing the cattle. Also you can tell them that there will be more cattle to cross in future as I know you and Simon want to make new stock route down by my land. I have already made a causeway for the cattle to cross the Galana.

With some alarm she realised she had finished stitching, but was still sitting very comfortably on his knee. Rather than draw attention to her impropriety she became all medical.

"The river water will be dirty. I think you should take penicillin for ten days to stop the wound going septic. I don't want my stitches to become infected, so I have to stitch you up again."

65

With a cheeky smile he replied, "That's a pity I rather enjoyed you sitting on lap."

Emily looked down and saw to her horror that she had not done all the buttons of her shirt up to her neck, and she was still only in her very skimpy bikini bottoms, not her more modest shorts. She blushed, but managed to say,

"I will forgive you as you are only a DC but I expect better behaviour when you become a PC!" Leonard chuckled as she got up. She suddenly remembered her training and asked,

"Are you up to date with your tetanus vaccination?" Leonard nodded.

"You are a very competent young lady. I'm glad you have come to my district, my province and indeed my country. I owe you more than my life. Thank you."

No more was said. He hugged her when Simon returned, and then he stood dominating the airstrip as they took off.

Once they were airborne and on a heading for Galana, Simon said,

"He is a great guy. He certainly took a shine to you!"

"I took a shine to him. I hope his head heals OK."

"I'm sure it will. Your stitching looked very neat." Emily said,

"Well thank you for my adventure. I really enjoyed the day. We are lucky people. I doubt if any two vets had as good fun as we have today and you are being paid for it!" Simon added ruefully,

"I don't take Cynthia out anymore or anyone else for that matter. I too have really enjoyed today. I thought you were amazing. I will have to buy you another bikini to replace today's."

"No need, Leonard's driver rinsed it out. When Johno has finished with it, it will look as good as new. Anyway knowing you, the next one will be even more revealing. There is not much of your present which you haven't seen! I forgot to tell you about my swimming pool near to my house which Colin built for me when he had some spare cement from the causeway. We had to make it with the big rocks in the river. It is really a deep rock pool. There is a small waterfall flowing into it and the water flows over a large flat rock at the other side. It is good fun lying in the shallow water and there is another flat bit which is normally dry for sunbathing. I'm sure the brown water gives me a better tan."

Simon could not stop himself stroking the top of her inner thigh, saying,

"I had noticed that you are brown up to your bikini bottoms."

Emily arched her back and made a quiet pouring noise. Simon realised what he was doing and immediately stopped, saying,

"I saw Ken before I flew off this morning. He said if I was here, even though it is not strictly legal that you could do an hour of local flying on your own around Galana to build up you hours." Emily sighed,

"Yes that would be good. Abdi will make you a cup of tea by the pool, or have you had enough of river water for the day. Do you want to stay for supper and leave early in the morning?" Simon replied,

"I would love that." They had an enjoyable evening.

Chapter 8

The Flying Exams

Monday 13th February 1967

Emily was sad the day of her written exam, as Simon said he was away in Nairobi, to be briefed about the new Foot and Mouth vaccination campaigns. He had gone up the night before on the overnight train and then was returning on the down train that night. Emily tried to suppress the little niggle that he had a girl, in Nairobi. She said to herself she was being ridiculous and anyhow it was up to him. He could have girls anywhere he liked. They were not an item.

She made the most of her time in Mombasa. She took Alex and Tuku. They picked up various stores while she had a lesson with Ken then she had her written flying exam. She was a little up scuttled as Simon had booked her in for her compulsory radio-telephony exam as well. However in fact she did know it all. Ken met her after the exam. They went quickly over the papers. Ken listened to her answers and said he thought she had passed without any problems. Then he asked if she wanted another lesson doing spins. Emily jumped at the idea. To get her PPL she needed to demonstrate to her instructor that she had got the plane out of a spin in a safe manner. The only thing she was worried about was that she would hurt Hattie by putting the wings under too much stress. As they got into the plane, she winked at Ken saying,

"My shorts are fairly long but my top is a little low. NO PEAKING. I want your total concentration on my flying and the instruments."

She took off and cleared with the tower that they were going to do some local flying. They climbed to five thousand feet. On the way Ken told her what was going to happen and what she had got to do.

Ken had good look around to make sure there were no other planes in the sky anywhere near them. He was flying, but she was following him with her hands and feet on the controls. When they were going straight and level he pulled back the stick hard into his tummy. Hattie climbed, but the climb was too steep for her. Her speed fell off rapidly. Emily knew Hattie had no stall warning noise. As she stalled, her nose dropped and Ken kicked on left rudder. She went into a spin. The ground whirled in front of her eyes, but Emily had not forgotten what he had told her to do. She pushed the stick forward as hard as she could and kicked on the opposite rudder to the spin. Immediately Hattie responded. The spinning stopped and her speed picked up, so that Emily could slowly pull her out of her dive. Ken said,

"Well done, look at your altimeter, you did well. You have only lost three hundred feet. However you must remember that, however good a pilot you are, you are going to lose altitude. Never do a spin near to the ground or you will die. You also did well, as you didn't try to bring her out off the dive too quickly. If you do that you can then go into what is called a high speed stall and you will lose altitude very quickly. A Tripacer is a very forgiving aircraft you just watch now."

He put Hattie in to a spin, but put his hand across to stop her reacting. Slowly the spinning stopped and then he let Emily pull her out of the dive. He said,

"See she came out herself. Lots of more modern aircraft will keep on spinning until they hit the ground." Emily said,

"Let's climb up again and have one more go. You never know. I may fall out of my top! Ken grinned,

"I would love to see that!"

This time Emily put Hattie into a spin and then got her out of it, again only losing three hundred feet. She said,

"Sorry Ken, my tits are too small they are still in my top." Ken added,

"They still look good to me."

When they had parked Hattie and were walking back to the aero club, Ken said,

"It's about time we fixed your flying test." Emily said,

69

"I have only done thirty seven hours including today. I need another three hours." Ken replied,

"Well I think you should arrange it now. You are on top form. You might start getting into bad habits. I will go with you for an hour before your test just to pull you up on any mistakes you are making. The test will take about an hour and a quarter so you then only have to do forty five minutes. The job will then be done. However promise me you won't get sloppy up there on your own at Galana."

"I promise Ken. I will be coming down to Mombasa pretty often. I love it in the wilds, but I do want a bit of a social life."

They went in and found Tom Dove in his office and fixed the test for the following Monday. Emily picked up Alex and Tuku and returned to Galana in high spirits. She did not see Simon and in fact did not speak to him, but heard him on the radio. He seemed to have a lot of work on so she did not call him up, although she was longing to.

There was plenty to do at Galana. Weekends did not mean much. She did do a bit of sunbathing in the middle of the day. Her body was used to the sun. It was great to spend just a few minutes and then cool off in her rock pool. She was sure all the staff thought she was totally mad. When she had a shower to wash off the river water, she was quite pleased with her tan marks. She had no marks on her back, just a small white bottom. She was sure she had caught some sun on her breasts on the Tana as they hardly seemed white now. She just had a sexy triangle down below. She longed to take off her clothes in front of Simon and see his reaction. She missed him particularly at the weekends, when she was sure he was having fun. She was just so envious of the girls in Mombasa would could give him the eye and just have fun with him, even if they didn't seduce him. She had no right to expect him not to be seduced or for that matter to do the seducing. She worried that she was just over sexed. Christopher Columbus she bloody wanted him.

On Sunday unless there was a panic on, there was no radio call. She was surprised he was not the radio on Monday morning but his staff seemed to be managing. Her lesson with Ken was at ten o'clock so she had to get going and did not really give it any more thought. Her flying exam went like a dream. Tom shook her by the hand and congratulated her. Now all she had to do was forty five minute flying and get him to sign her log book. She decided to do the flying there and then, as he said he would be staying up at the airport. She had a great flight, flying down the beach on the South Coast and then coming back over the Shimba Hills Game Park.

Once she had sorted out all the paper work and put her log book and forms into the post to go to the Civil Aviation Authority in Nairobi she was about to drive back to Galana when she thought dam it, I feel like a celebration. If Simon isn't at home, I will leave him a note and go and have a meal at the Chini Club. If the worst comes to the worst and he is taking out some girl I will stay the night at the Chini Club and drive back to Galana in the morning. She knew the office closed at four o'clock so he might be home. Jonathan would know if he had gone sailing or water skiing. He had told her that rugger training did not really start until the beginning of April. She swung into his drive and was pleased to see his Landrover in its normal place in the shade. There was no sign of Jonathan in the back kitchen so she walked into the house. She immediately heard a moaning sound from upstairs and a voice talking. She thought, '*Oh no, he is making love to some girl.*' She was about to make a swift exit and in fact she was so strung up she was nearly in tears, when her strong side took over. She thought, '*Well it will stop me mooning about if I actually know he is shagging someone else.*' With that she called out at the bottom of the stairs,

"Hello. Is anyone at home?" The moaning continued as she climbed the stairs, calling again,

"Hello." Somehow the moaning did not sound like lovemaking, so she continued up the stairs. His bedroom door was open. Bravely she went in. He was naked on the bed in a muck sweat moaning and tossing from side to side. He obviously had a high fever. She ran to him and held his shoulders. He was delirious. He did not recognise her. She kept trying to wake him. She ran to the bathroom and got a cold wet flannel to mop his brow. Then she thought, '*This is no good.*' She got a towel and soaked it in cold water and laid it on his body. He was so hot he seemed to be burning up. He was still sweating. He suddenly grabbed her. He was so strong she could not get him to release her. It was at that moment when Ian and Jonathan came in. If Emily had not been so worried about Simon she would have been terribly embarrassed, as with Simon naked they certainly

71

looked in a compromising position. However she had no need to be worried on that score. Jonathan had seen how ill Simon was and had run to get the doctor. Ian had given him a lift back in his car.

Ian then took charge as they prized open Simon's arms from around her. Jonathan and Emily held Simon down as Ian gave him an injection of Chloroquine, as he was certain Simon had Malaria. Apparently to Ian's knowledge, Simon had never had Malaria before, which was why he was so ill now. With difficulty they got Simon into a towel robe and then Jonathan with Emily's help got him downstairs as Ian got the back of his car ready with the back seats folded down. There was no point in calling an ambulance, as they were so near to the Katherine Bibby Hospital. Emily thought Ian was marvellous in the hospital as he organised everything. Simon was put in a single room. He still did not recognise anyone, but he was much quieter and had stopped sweating. Ian said it was fine if Emily wanted to stay with Simon, but she should not exhaust herself, as they had staff to cope with this sort of thing. Jonathan had walked home to sort the house out. Ian left saying he would look in around ten before he went home to bed. Emily sat by Simon's bedside, wishing she could do something to make him better. Dreadful thoughts of him dying of cerebral malaria kept popping into her mind. She was cross with herself for thinking that he had been making love to some rival. She prayed for him to survive particularly, when suddenly his teeth started to chatter and he moaned that he was so cold. She wrapped her arms around him and he dropped off into a fitful sleep. Then she must have dozed off as Ian gently woke her saying,

"Emily, you go back to Simon's house and get some sleep. He is asleep now and his temperature is almost down to normal. Hopefully the crisis is over. Come back in the morning. I will look in on my way to the surgery."

So with some reluctance Emily left and walked to Simon's home. It was the same path that they had followed on New Year's Night. It seemed so long ago, but in fact it was only three months. Emily felt completely drained. Jonathan was still up and he insisted he made her some food and a cup of tea. He had been away for the weekend and had returned to find Simon ill on Sunday night. Simon had then deteriorated until he got into the state in which Emily had found him.

Emily ate the food, wished Jonathan goodnight, had a quick shower and was soon asleep, totally exhausted.

She awoke and initially did not know where she was. Then she realised she was in Simon's house and a smile lit up her face, only to be dashed, when she remembered how ill he was. She leapt out of bed and nearly collided with Jonathan bringing her tea. She was totally naked, but nothing fazed her. She shouted her thanks as she went into the shower. She was glad she had left some clothes here as yesterdays were very dirty. Jonathan like Abdi was a marvel. Everything was beautifully washed and ironed, even her knickers. She did not want to stop for breakfast, but she thought it was so rude to Jonathan if she didn't. She told him she would go to the hospital immediately. She ran out the door. In fact she was glad of breakfast. She had been hungry and had no idea when or where she would get her next meal.

She was before Ian at the hospital. The night sister was just about to go off duty. Emily asked her about Simon. Apparently he was now lucid, but was very weak. He could not sit up on his own. The sister said normally visitors were not allowed to see patients before the doctor had been, however she would let Emily in, as she knew how close she was to the patient. Emily thought, *'Not as close as I want to be. Thank God he is still alive.'* Then she burst into tears. The sister was very experienced and could see her distress. Sadly having worked all her career in the tropics she had seen many tragedies. The sister put her arm around Emily,

"Take your time and compose yourself. You won't be doing him any favours in tears." Emily's stronger side immediately came to the fore.

"Thank you sister. I should be stronger. I'm a vet like the patient."

The sister squeezed her shoulders,

"I know all about you both."

Even in her emotional state, Emily wondered how this girl knew so much. Had she had a fling with Simon? Emily blew her nose and wiped her eyes thanking her lucky stars that she had not bothered with any make up. She went into the room conscious that the sister had followed her in. Emily was very shocked. Simon looked like a corpse. He was as white as a sheet and his eyes were sunken. She had not expected him to be so still, having seen him in such a state yesterday. She walked to the bed and took his hand. She gave it a gentle squeeze, but there was no movement of his hand. She could just see his gentle breathing. However she could tell he was awake as his eyes flickered. She longed to kiss him, but knew that might upset him and the last thing she wanted was a scene in front of the sister. She managed to say,

"Poor you, you have been very ill, but you are getting better." She had to lean close to hear him,

"Can you take charge now, and get on the radio." He gave a dreadful sigh and she thought for one dreadful moment that he had died. Then she saw him take a breath. She replied,

"Of course, I will get to work. I'm not very good at this Florence Nightingale stuff." She just saw him nod his head slightly. She turned to the sister and said,

"He is worried about his work. I will leave him in your good care and go immediately to his office and get on the radio as that's what he wants."

The sister was surprised, but did not show it. She had thought that Emily was a weak, wilting violet. She now realised her mistake. This young lady was very professional and decisive.

Emily ran back to Simon's house. Her shirt was soaking with sweat, but she did not care. She quickly told Jonathan what was happening. She jumped into her Landrover and roared off to the veterinary office. Would she be in time before the missionaries came on? She burst into Simon's outer office. His lovely old, grey haired, PA said,

"Good morning, Miss Emily. The PVO is not in yet." Emily knew she was gabbling,

"Mr Silas I know, he is in hospital. I must get on the radio. He is so terribly sick, but that was his only instruction."

"Of course, Miss Emily please enter his office." Emily marvelled, how just because she was a European everything was OK. She had absolutely no right to go in the office. She went to the radio. Mercifully it was all set up. She switched it on. Immediately she heard a very desperate voice,

"PVO Coast, this is District Livestock Officer (DLO) Mandera. I am at El Wak. I have a big problem." Emily replied,

"I am acting for PVO Coast. Go ahead with your problem. Over."
She was desperately thinking, '*Where the hell is El Wak.*' Then she
remembered it was far up North right on the Somali border.

"Cattle are ill to the East of the town. It looks like Foot and
Mouth Disease (FMD), but it is unusual as the cattle are dying. Over
fifty of the mob of one hundred, are already dead. What are your
instructions?" Emily remembered her disease control lectures, but
she had never been told about cross country border control.

"Are the cattle actually in Kenya or are they in Somalia? Over."
Oh she wished she had time to think.

"They are outside of the town, so I suppose they are still in
Somalia." Emily thought, '*I'm sure Simon would know what to do.*'
She felt a tear trickle down her face as she thought, '*He might have
died.*' She replied,

"What is your name DLO Mandera? I am called Emily, over"

"I know who you are. You saved the DC Galole's life in the Tana.
I am called Mbogwa, over." Emily replied with more confidence,

"Right Mr. Mbogwa. These are my specific instructions until I
can get up to you later today. I will fly in to El Wak airstrip. I will
buss the town for you to meet me. Do you copy that?"

"Yes I will meet you. What about the cattle? Over."

"This is very important. The cattle are NOT to enter Kenya on
any account. Use the District Officer and the Police if necessary. Do
you copy over."

"I copy that, Mbogwa out."

Emily now had a mission. If she was not any good at nursing
Simon back to life, she could at least take away his worries. First she
needed to reassure him. She went into the outer office to talk to Silas.
Instead she met an older European. He greeted her with,

"Hello, what brings you here? Simon never allows any of his girls
to come to the office."

Mr Silas cleared his throat and turned to Emily and said,

"I'm sorry Miss Emily. Mr. Ingram is the Port Veterinary Officer
he has been on extended compassionate home leave." Emily could
not stop herself scowling, but she held out her hand saying first to Mr
Silas,

"Thank you, Mr Silas. I would be very grateful if you could carry
out a very important and sensitive job for me. Could you take a

vehicle and a driver to the Katherine Bibby Hospital? There you will find Dr. Ian. McLeod. Can you tell him to brief The PVO, that he can relax as all is well at the office and at all the veterinary out-stations."

She turned to Mr. Ingram and she said,

"I think it would be best if you made yourself rather scarce, when the PVO comes back to the office. I doubt he will think very kindly of you saying I'm one of his girls. I understand they are always very glamorous. I am just a working rancher and I am seriously busy. Good day."

She strode out of the office.

She knew time was tight if she wanted to get back that night. She drove straight to Mombasa airport. She knew Hattie was fuelled up, as she had done it on the previous afternoon. However she knew she would need extra fuel. She also knew it was illegal, but she intended to carry extra fuel in four gallon cans. Simon had told her all the pilots did it when travelling big distances in the NFD. She loaded up the extra fuel on to Hattie's back seats. She took a water bottle and a four gallon plastic jerry can of water together with her rather meagre, compared to Simon's, veterinary kit out of the Landrover. Luckily she had an emergency supply of biscuits, she had learnt that chocolate was useless as it melted in minutes in the heat of the NFD. She also noticed she had a couple of oranges and a bag of cashew nuts in the Landrover. She took them. Then she filed her three and a quarter hour flight plan and set off. It was only when she was on the correct Northerly and slightly Western heading to El Wak that she had time to worry about Simon.

She thought, '*Oh God please don't let him die. I know I love him so much. Why was she doing all this? Was it to prove to him that she loved him? She doubted if he would see it that way. Was it to prove to him that she would make a better girl friend than some sexy married girl or air hostess? Did he actually want a girl friend? Did he just want a bit of undemanding sex? He certainly had made it clear to her that he did not want that from her. He had said he wanted a friend. So she was doing this to help him as a friend, nothing more.*'

Bang. She jumped and pushed the stick forward. *What the hell was that? Was Hattie going to blow up?* She had purposely climbed

76

really steadily to conserve fuel. She was now at six thousand feet she could lean the mixture out to conserve yet more fuel.

Bang. The same noise again. *It must be something to do with the engine. Had she leaned out the mixture too much? Oh Simon I need you so much.*

There were four more bangs, but still Hattie ran nice and evenly. She was now at ten thousand feet. She levelled off. She had registered that she had flown over the Galana. Now she could see the Tana. She was much further North than Garsen. She was even sure that she was further North than Galole, Leonard's home. He was certainly going to be another rock in her life, liked she wanted Simon to be, but she wanted Simon to be more. She wanted him to love her as a woman. She thought, *'There is no point in brooding over that. What in heaven's name were those bangs? At least they had stopped. Why were there six.'* Then it hit her. She had six extra tin petrol cans. They were expanding.

At least she had something to amuse Simon with, *'Keep fighting my darling. He would be so cross if could hear her wishes. Would he? He had never actually ever got cross with her. He was always kind to her. It was just he did not like her doing anything physical to him like kissing him. Perhaps he was gay! No way! He had enjoyed shagging Cynthia and Eve she was sure. Maybe he had even enjoyed shagging the sister at the hospital. If it would save him from death, Emily was happy for him to be shagging her right now. No she was certain he was not gay.* She remembered wistfully, him holding her so close on New Year's night. That made her hot. Then she thought of him stroking her inner thigh above the tan line of her shorts. Bloody hell that was good. It made her hotter still.

She must calm down and decide what she was going to do at El Wak. First she must see the cattle and make a diagnosis. She knew in her heart with her limited knowledge that FMD did not kill Zebu cattle and these were certainly Zebu cattle. Simon had told her there was no tick borne disease as far North as this. Also she was pretty certain there were no Tsetse fly to spread Trypanosomiasis. Simon had told her that Contagious Bovine Pleural Pneumonia (CBPP) was a constant worry. However she thought the LO would have been told about the respiratory signs. They would be pretty obvious. CBPP was a killer. However it killed animals slowly. Mr. Mbogwa had said they were dying in large numbers. It must be Rinderpest. Luckily she did remember the film she had been shown at college. There were dreadful rotting mouth lesions. It was much more serious than FMD. The cattle had very high temperatures. They showed excessive lacrimation and violent diarrhoea. The latter was common in calves all over the world with other infectious diseases, but it was rare in adult range cattle. She must look to see if they had the Z brand of Rinderpest vaccination, although this was only relevant for Kenya cattle. She must do a Post Mortem (PM). That would tell her. The zebra markings on the mucosa in the rectum were pathognomic, meaning that Rinderpest was the only disease to show this PM finding.

She looked down and the earth looked a dull tan colour. It was totally featureless. She looked at her watch. She should be reaching El Wak in half an hour, it was time to use her height to gain speed. Her active thoughts had made the journey go quicker. She was down to a thousand feet when she estimated she was fifteen minutes out. Thank goodness, there was the strip, she was dead on. She put Hattie's nose down. Her speed soon picked up as the altimeter slowly unwound. She called on the radio in case there was another aircraft in the vicinity. There was silence. She lost more height and decided to come straight in. She did not want to enter the airspace of Somalia. Now she could see the town. It was very small, but was dominated by an old fashioned Arabic fort. She did not think she needed to buss the town. She could see three Landrovers with dust streams, heading for the airstrip. Down went full flap, she cut the power, she was too high, but Ken had often said to her, it was better to crash at ten miles an hour into the far end of the field than crash at seventy miles an hour if you were too low at the near end of the field.

Hattie swooped down like an eagle. The strip was easily long enough. She was down, coming to a halt with four hundred yards to spare. That gave her more confidence as she got out of the plane. A man in ordinary clothes greeted her,

"Welcome Miss Emily I am Mbogwa, I am pleased to introduce Mr. Kimathi the DO and Chief Inspector Koiigy." The DO was obviously the most senior.

"We are all grateful for your prompt action and are sorry to hear the PVO is in hospital. However we have this serious problem. A

Kenyan national had agreed to buy one hundred cattle from a Somali trader. On the way here the cattle started to die. There are now only twenty two left. The Kenya national does not want the cattle. The Somali trader is not happy. On your instructions this morning, we have not let the cattle in to Kenya. My Askaris and the police are guarding the border. We await your instructions. Emily's heart was in her mouth. She knew what she had to do, but was terribly afraid. "First of all I am not a Kenyan Government Officer unlike all of you. I don't want any of you to get into trouble or to cause a possible international incident. Therefore I will go on my own with my sampling equipment and see the cattle. I would be grateful if one of you could give me a lift so I am within walking distance of the border. Also Chief Inspector I would be grateful if you could mount a guard on my plane. They all smiled. The DO said,

"That's what we will do. I'm sure my colleagues will pray for your safety, as I will. We already know of your bravery." Emily nodded and followed the DO to his Landrover. She carried her small veterinary bag.

They only had to drive half a mile into the town and then a further mile out East across the dry scrub. '*At least her Galana had Acacia trees and some sparse grass.*' As she got out of the Landrover she said to the DO,

"I suggest you and the others return to the town. It will be less confrontational if I am seen to be all alone. You will be able to see from the fort when I return." The DO did not give her much encouragement by saying,

"God be with you."

As she set off she mused, '*That the DO was talking about a Christian God. She suspected, as she entered Somalia a Moslem God would be more powerful.*' She had never felt more alone until she remembered her first morning, when Abdi had taken her in to see Auntie Mary's corpse. Simon had arrived to save her. Now she was just a small girl, totally alone.

She could see the thorn cattle boma. She walked on. She could see the vultures circling. Would they be eating her soon? There were only five men at the boma, all dressed in white galabiers. Emily nodded and said in English,

"I am sorry to hear of your loss."

She was worried that she should have greeted them first in Swahili, with, Hello, How are you. Then she was shocked by a very Oxford Accent.

"Thank you for coming so quickly. I will speak for my father. He understands English but does not speak it so well." Emily then noticed the older man who had some few grey hairs, but stood tall. The younger man continued,

"The Kenyan's will have told you their side of the story. Are you a Government Veterinary Officer? I am surprised, as I did not think ODA recruited women." Emily smiled and said,

"Shall I tell you the truth?" The old man said something in what Emily took for Somali. The young man translated,

"My father said, most of the time the British men do speak the truth, but he has never spoken to a British women before. So do carry on."

"I am a private vet. I had a passion as a young girl to come to Africa. As you rightly say, the ODA do not recruit women particularly little ones." The old man said a couple of words. The young Somali said,

"My father says that they certainly do not recruit beautiful girls like you." Emily just bowed her head to him and continued,

"I despaired until I got a letter from my Aunt who owned Galana ranch asking me to come and help her. I arrived three months ago. She died of a heart attack the night I arrived. I was helped by the Kenyan PVO. I have been running the ranch ever since. I have fallen in love with the PVO. He is fighting for his life in hospital. His wish, which may be was his dying wish was, that the Coast and the North East Provinces' Veterinary Services should continue to be run properly. I am the best person to carry out his wishes." The one tear which ran down her cheek was not missed by her audience.

The old man said a few words. The young Somali said,

"Father said, to thank you being so honest. Now we will show you the cattle."

They walked into the boma. Emily could see at a glance that none of them had the Z brand of Rinderpest vaccination. Also many of the cattle were showing signs, as she had seen in the film at college. She was taken to an animal which presumably had recently died. A crude PM had been performed. The lungs were normal. The rectum had been cut open and displayed the classic zebra markings. Emily thought, '*These guys know what they are doing!*'

She turned to the old man and said,

"These cattle are dying of Rinderpest. I suggest you slaughter the remaining animals. Any which do not have a fever may be sold as meat. Do you mind if I take some samples to confirm my diagnosis but I am certain I'm correct." The old man nodded his head.

She took samples quickly from the corpse and got two live sick animals held for her. She took blood from their jugulars. They all walked out of the boma. The old man said something, as Emily shook his hand, as she said goodbye. All the men laughed. The young man said, "My father salutes you. He says he hopes the PVO knows, that he, my father values you at a thousand camels, your father should not part with you for less!" She was just about to turn and leave but said,

"If it is not rude, where did you learn your excellent English?" The young man smiled,

"I studied at Oxford. I think I was chosen as I used to be quite quick over ten thousand metres!" Emily answered with a smile,

"That is a bit far for me. I could only manage a two twenty." The old man said something in Somali. The young man explained before he translated. My father meant this as a joke he said,

"That's lucky as the border is less than that distance. We will give you half a minute before we start shooting!" She replied,

"My father will sad if he can't collect his thousand camels." The old man said in English.

"God go with you."

Emily turned and set off walking towards the fort across the desert. She could hear the old man chuckling. When she had gone five hundred yards she was met by the DO's Landrover. He seemed very relieved to see her. At the plane were the other Kenyans. She explained that the cattle had got Rinderpest. She was certain, but she had taken samples to confirm her diagnosis. She said they definitely had not been vaccinated in Kenya. She said that they were going to slaughter the remaining cattle that day and she doubted they would hear any more about it. She said she thought it was best if they did not say anything more to anyone. She made them laugh, as she asked if they could bring two Landrovers under the planes high wings so she could fill up the fuel tanks, as she was too short. As it was the drivers did it for her. She shook everyone's hands and said goodbye.

It was a long boring flight home, but she thought she had a tail wind which would get her home a little quicker. It was going to be a near thing to beat the dark. She thought about Simon. Hopefully he was a little better. Ian had been fairly upbeat the previous night, but perhaps that was only to get her to go home. At least Simon could relax about the Coast Province and the stock route. Now she had to work out what she had to do now with the information she had that Rinderpest was active on the Kenyan border and what to do with the samples. One thing she was certain of was that she was not going to say anything on the radio for the entire world to hear. Also there was no way she was going to involve that idiot My Ingram.

Officially she had landed it in the dark as it was a minute after 7 pm. She only got a very mild rebuke from the tower, "Cutting it a little fine, Alpha Tango!"

She was now bone tired, but wanted to go to the hospital as quickly as she could, so she did not bother to fill up Hattie. She then had the sense to go to Simon's house first to put the samples in the fridge, then to shower and change before walking at a sensible pace to the hospital. Ian had left, but the same sister was back on duty. Emily was so relieved that the sister said that Simon was still holding his own. She led her to his room. Then Emily nearly despaired. He was just the same as in the morning. She had not really understood 'holding his own'. Actually he was asleep and was just softly breathing. She gently took his hand. It was ice cold. He did not wake. Emily turned and beckoned the sister out of the room.

"Has he woken much during the day?" She replied,

"Not much, but that's for the best as the last thing we want is for him to be delirious." Emily knew all about him being delirious.

"Did Mr. Silas give my message to Dr. Macleod?"

"Do you mean the very polite, kind, man from the Veterinary Department? My colleague saw him talking to Dr. Macleod who came straight into see and talk to the patient." Emily breathed out with a sigh,

"Thank Goodness for that. I am going to leave you now and go back home to make an important telephone call to the Veterinary Department. If I may I will come back later."

Chapter 9

Emily Meets the DVS

Emily left. She just hoped she could trust the staff. The last thing she wanted was for either of the sisters to say anything untoward to Simon if he should wake. Equally she did not want this sister particularly, to think she was going out on the town, not caring about Simon. She walked home with a heavy heart. Jonathan like a guardian angel had made her supper. She did not realise how hungry she was. Then she looked on Simon's personal telephone directory for the home number of the Director of Veterinary Services (DVS). She noticed several girls' names and smiled. What were they to her? Simon had admitted he was, in his words, 'a rake'. She found the Nairobi number and rang. She was surprised, as she understood there was usually a minimum delay of thirty minutes to Nairobi, but it was ringing immediately. She thought, '*That information must be during the day.*' However she was flustered, but controlled herself as a very abrupt voice said,

"Horatio Ngugi."

"I'm sorry to ring you at home and in the evening, but I'm a veterinary surgeon and I have some extremely important information. My name is Emily Barrington-Long. I arrived in Kenya just before Christmas."

"Yes, I remember the name. Simon Longfield the PVO Coast recommended you very highly for immediate registration, as a veterinary surgeon. How can I help you?" Emily did not beat about the bush. This African obviously did not suffer fools gladly.

"I have just come from the hospital. Simon is critically ill with what could be cerebral malaria. He is holding his own, but was delirious last night. He could barely speak this morning, but he stressed to me to make sure the Coast Province and the stock route were in order. I got on the radio to receive a radio call from the DLO

Madera who was at El Wak. That is on the Somali border North of Wajir." The voice snapped back,

"I'm well aware of the vicinity of El Wak. Why were you as a private veterinary surgeon using a government radio net work?" With icy control, Emily kept her cool,

"I am the owner of Galana ranch and I have a license to use two radios on the net work."

"You are not licensed to carry out Government business!"

"My ranch has agreed to cooperate with the Government to build a new stock route south from the Tana to the Galana."

"Very well, what has that got to do with El Wak?" Emily blundered on,

"The LO reported that Somali cattle were dying in some numbers just outside of Kenya near to El Wak. He wanted the PVOs advice. I knew he was too ill to speak, let alone give advice. I told the LO to make sure the cattle did not enter Kenya and to use the DO and the police to enforce that if necessary." The voice was seriously angry now.

"Do I understand correctly that you gave instructions to one of my staff?" Emily replied,

"Yes."

"Well at least you are honest. Why did you not contact me?"

"I only had a couple of minute's air time left. There is a minimum of half an hour delay with calls from Mombasa to Nairobi."

"So what did you do then?"

"I flew up to El Wak. I met the DLO, the DO and the Chief Inspector. I walked alone into Somalia. I examined the Cattle. Only twenty remained out of one hundred. None had the Rinderpest Vaccination brand. I did a PM and can confirm Rinderpest. I have taken samples which are now in the fridge here. I told the Somali trader to slaughter the rest." A very sarcastic voice then said,

"I assume you weren't shot in the back, as you are speaking to me now. Well at least you used your head and kept the disease out of Kenya. Have you been on the radio?"

"No. I told them to keep their mouths shut."

"Well if what you say is true, you have my admiration. Who will pay for this safari, heaven only knows. Will the pilot keep his mouth shut?"

84

"I flew myself in my own plane. The PVO was very kind to me when I first arrived on Galana Ranch and my Aunt died that night. I owe it to him. There will be no expense to the Department."

"Well on the face of it you have potentially saved the Department and the Country considerable embarrassment and also saved our very lucrative beef export markets. Therefore I authorise you to fly the samples up to Kabete, at the Department's expense. I will send a car to the aero club at Wilson airport. It will wait for you from ten o'clock. Do not say anything to anyone. Come straight with the samples to my office. I hope to God the PVO gets better quickly." Emily suspected he did not hear her reply of, "So do I." He had put the phone down.

She slumped down in the chair. Jonathan must have heard the call end, as he brought her in a cup of coffee. She thanked him and said she was sorry to bother him, but if he could make breakfast at 5.30 am tomorrow she could call and see Simon and then fly to Nairobi. She said she would go and see Simon now after she had drunk her coffee before going to bed. Once again she was a sad lonely girl walking to the hospital.

She actually missed the tranquillity of Galana. The slow old river had a very soothing effect. She knew no news was good news. She hoped they would come on the radio tomorrow. She had left instructions that if there was a real drama then Julius was to send down Christmas with either the lorry or the Landrover.

The hospital was very quiet. There was no sign of the Sister. So she went to Simon's room. He was still asleep. She sat in a chair beside him and held his hand. She must have gone to sleep as she woke with a start with Simon shouting,

"Where am I? Who's looking after the Stock route?" He grabbed her hand. Emily said,

"Simon its Emily. The stock route is fine. You are in hospital." He still gripped her hand,

"Emily, Emily, you found me. I tried to hold you. You tried to run away. I frightened you. I was naked." He still held her hand in a vice like grip.

"Don't run away. Cynthia means nothing to me."

At that moment the sister came in. Simon shouted,

"Don't let Emily run away. I won't hurt her." The sister said in a soothing voice,

"Don't worry Simon. I won't let Emily leave. Just relax. Lie back and let go of her hand."

Simon gave a deep sigh and relaxed. Then he seemed to lose consciousness. Emily looked at the Sister and mouthed I must have fallen asleep. The sister looked at her watch. She obviously had been asleep in her office and felt guilty.

"It's nearly midnight. You should not be here." It was on the tip of Emily's tongue to say, but you should have been here, but she let it ride. Instead she said,

"I will leave you now and go to his house. Can you ring me there, if you have any problems? I will return early in the morning. I have to fly out early after I have seen Simon, to give a progress report to the Director of Veterinary Services." It was as near to the truth as Emily was prepared to go.

The sister said,

"What's his house telephone number?" Emily could not resist saying,

"Oh I thought you had it. Yours was on his list of private numbers." Then she relented,

"I'm sorry to be so bitchy. It's just he means so very much to me. Please look after him. I'm torn by wanting to be with him, and carrying out his wishes to keep his blasted job going." The sister replied,

"Are you his new flame?"

"No I am not, but I owe him for all his kindness when my Auntie Mary died suddenly on the night, when I first arrived." The sister replied,

"I see, you go and get some sleep. You look all in." Emily thought, *thanks for that. I suppose I should not have been so bitchy. You can have his affection. Just make him well again.*' She left without another word. She walked back to Simon's house a very worried girl. She thought she would not sleep because she was worrying so much about Simon. However the sister was right, she was all in. It was so hot that even with the big old fan turning rapidly, she fell into a deep sleep, naked on top of the sheet. She only woke with Jonathan's discrete cough in the doorway with her tea.

She was mortified. She could not find her kikoi and just grabbed the top sheet to hide her modesty. Somehow being totally naked embarrassed her much more that just having bare breasts, like with Leonard. As she was cleaning her teeth she thought the reason was that actually she was very proud of her breasts. They were quite noticeable, as she was so slender. They were very firm and did not sag. Men were always looking which actually pleased her rather than annoying her.

She dressed in her smartest shirt and trousers and ate her breakfast quickly. She thanked Jonathan and said she would be back for supper. She would go to see Simon before she flew up to Nairobi.

The same sister was still on duty. They eyed each other warily. Emily was relieved that Simon was quietly sleeping. She asked the sister to tell him all was normal at the Veterinary Office, but she was not confident the message would be passed on. Emily consoled herself that at least he was not delirious.

Emily did not stop at the Veterinary Office. She was too early for the radio call. She would do it, when she was airborne and had plenty of height to give good reception. The control tower gave her clearance for immediate take off as, although it was hardly light, there were no other aircraft in the Mombasa control zone. It worked well, as she had gained over five thousand feet before she changed frequencies to get on to the stock route radio call. All was well on the stock route. There was just routine ordering of stores and information of cattle movement. She wrote down all the messages on a pad strapped to her knee. She smiled as today she was wearing trousers. She would have looked ridiculous in short shorts, but Ken would have certainly had his eye on her thighs. She was pleased that in the past she remembered Simon having quick looks.

She was very relieved when Julius came on and reported that all was well at Galana. Just before the missionaries were due to come on she was annoyed that Mr Ingram, she had not been told his Christian name, came on. He had obviously just arrived at the office and switched on. He said in a rather off hand way that the PVO was not at the office. Emily immediately chipped in angrily.

"I have just come from the hospital. He is still critical, but is holding his own. I have made a note of the routine matters and will call into the office on my return from Kabete. Galana out!"

Emily was relieved that she didn't have to elaborate as the missionaries started their very tedious chatty round up.

She changed frequency and concentrated on flying. Visibility was good. There was no low stratus cloud over the Machakos hills. She thought about the arrogant rancher who farmed there who thought that flying was a pointless exercise just because he couldn't do it. He would have only been a quarter of the way to El Wak if he had been trying to do what she had done. He might be good looking, but Emily thought, '*If I can't have Simon, I would much rather be on my own.*'

She contacted Nairobi control after she had signed off from East Air Centre. They told her to continue and report overhead the visual marker. She had never flown into Wilson before. She found the visual marker on the map, but was in a panic, when she couldn't find it on the ground. After five minutes, but what felt like an hour, she blagged it and reported,

"Alpha Tango reporting the visual marker."

She was told to report long finals. Obviously there were many students learning, as she was told there were seven in the circuit. Once again she was nervous, as she could only see three of them. Then she reported long finals. She hoped that, as she was inbound from Mombasa they would give her some priority. She did not relish going round in the busy unusual right hand circuit. She was told she was finals number five. Where were they all? She could only see two! Then she saw them all. She was looking in the wrong place. The missing two were actually close together over the Runway and the Langata Road. She saw two planes land and take off again and one was told to overshoot. There was one ahead of her. Luckily Hattie had a low landing speed. Emily increased the flap and then cut the power to compensate. It was going to be tight. The aircraft in front landed and took off again as she crossed the Langata road. She was cleared to land. With some relief she cut the power and flared out to land. She floated further than she would have liked, but made a smooth landing in time for the second turn out, rather than the third and final turn out. The tower told her she had landed at 9.55. She was on time. She rather thought Horatio would like people to be on time.

She parked at the aero club as the green, veterinary staff car pulled into the car park. She left her navigation stuff, emergency food and water and just took her small hand bag and the small cooler bag with the samples out of the plane. She locked the door and walked to the waiting car. The driver smartly jumped out and held the rear passenger door for her. Emily smiled,

"I would rather ride in front with you."

"Certainly Miss Emily." It was interesting that this name had stuck, rather than her long-winded surname, and that he had been given it. She asked his name,

"Boniface." Was his reply. Emily laughed,

"Luckily your face matches your name. My face was very cross when I was woken so early in the morning to get here!" It was Boniface's turn to laugh,

"All my children have happy faces." On the twenty minute journey they talked about his wife and his four children. When they arrived at the impressive office block at the Veterinary Laboratories, Boniface drew up in front of the main door. Emily did not realise but she was being observed by the Director's PA. He went into the director's office and reported,

"The lady has arrived on time she is chatting to the driver." Horatio's eyebrows rose. He had not thought she would be a woman to chat to a driver. When she was shown into his office, he was even more surprised. He said rather rudely, but Emily took it as honesty,

"I did not expect someone so young and pretty." Emily added,

"And so small."

"Well yes." Emily took an instant liking to him and smiled warmly. Horatio continued.

"I will admit that I have been checking up on you after our conversation last night. The President's office had heard about you." Emily's eye brows shot up. Horatio tried to put her at her ease adding.

"The President's office is responsible for all the PCs, the DCs and the DOs. There is a glowing report from the new PC at the coast and the PC at Garissa has a report from his DO at El Wak to say he was totally amazed with your bravery, as he feared for your life. The Ministry of Agriculture found an application for employment from you last year. It seems you were treated very unfairly by your ODA. They did not recommend your appointment on account of your gender and stature. I stress that was your government not mine. However now you have got to give me a serious explanation of your action and conduct. However I have been very remiss. What news of my PVO?"

"I called into the hospital on my way to the Airport. He was stable and sleeping which is a relief as he was delirious when I went to see him after I had spoken to you." Horatio looked at her keenly,

"Are you in a relationship with the PVO?" Emily looked him in the eye.

"I am not sure you have the right to ask a lady such a question?"

"However I am sure, even with your offer of help to the Government with the construction of a stock route, that you do not have the right to meddle in the affairs of My Department." All the while Emily had looked him in the eye. She had not looked down. She replied simply,

"Touché!" He said,

"Are you going to honestly answer my question? The PVO Coast knows that I will not allow the mixing of Government Work and pleasure." Emily knew then some of Simon's problem with her. She answered,

"I will answer your question as honestly as I can, but it is with a large amount of reluctance and I am putting you on trust that you will keep this information confidential. We have a strictly business relationship. We are good friends and enjoy each other's company. Simon has been very kind and helpful to me. However I have not told anyone else, but I am in love with him." The DVS queried,

"You have not told Simon?" Emily answered,

"Certainly NOT Simon!" Horatio smiled,

"Your feelings are safe with me. Even grey haired old Africans were young once." He was, although he hated to admit it, very touched, when she stepped forward and hugged him saying,

"I am so terribly worried about him. He really is in a critical condition." Horatio replied,

"I also am worried, as I have important plans for him in the department and I expect you to keep that confidential and in your words to tell no one, particularly NOT Simon!"

Emily knew then that they, not only had an understanding, but also liked each other. She was flabbergasted when they broke apart and he said,

"Regardless of your Government, I would like to offer you a job as a field veterinary officer. However it is only in my power to offer you local terms. It is up to the British Government to give you proper and rightful overseas terms." Emily was still shocked, but blurted out,

"I would very much like to take you up on your offer, although the British appear to be very unfair." The DVS replied,

"I can at least give you some more money and the authority which I'm sure by your behaviour you deserve. The job I am offering you will be hard, but I am convinced you can do it as well as run your ranch, where I consider you will not be working to your full potential. I want you to take a new post of PVO North Eastern Province. I want ever bovine animal in that province vaccinated against Rinderpest without delay. I have funds available through the Food and Agricultural Organisation (FAO) under my direct control. You will be based at Garissa." He added with a wry smile,

"Garissa is a town further up the Tana than Galole." Emily laughed,

"In your words, I am well aware of the vicinity of Garissa!" They both laughed together then. The DVS finished then saying,

"The bloody paper work will take forever, but I want you in post with immediate effect. You will have to liaise with the PC North Eastern Province and his staff. You will have three District Livestock Officers under you. You have already met the DLO Mandera. Good luck. I know you will do a good job. Now come with me for a cup of coffee and I will introduce you to some of the laboratory staff. My PA will discretely take the samples to the correct laboratory."

The DVS was good to his word. Obviously he was not really liked that much by the other staff except the older more senior staff. Emily was thankful she had got on so well with him. The more junior vets were visibly frightened of him. Emily was also aware that Simon must have had very rapid promotion as he was in a similar grade to much more senior laboratory vets.

All the vets, both young and old were horrified that she had been posted to Garissa. All of them would have loathed to have been sent there. However Emily enjoyed meeting them as many said they needed samples from her province. She said that they were very welcome to stay with her either in Garissa when she had got settled or right away at Galana. She made them all laugh describing her muddy swimming pool.

Boniface gave her a ride back to Wilson, but just as she was about to get in the car a very young European came running up to her. He introduced himself. He was a Swiss vet who was working for the FAO. He had been given a house at Kabete. He had been tasked to investigate and indeed carry out the new Rinderpest vaccination in North Eastern Province. He had been given a radio which he had yet to set up, but he was meant to liaise with the Livestock Marketing Division (LMD).

Emily knew instantly that he would be a great asset to her both here at Kabete and in the field. He enthused about going on Safari. She left him saying to him,

"Get that radio set up as soon as possible. Then we can chat easily. I suggest you set it up in your bedroom as we start early! What is your name? I'm Emily." He replied,

"Peter. I will fix it up this afternoon." Emily added,

"My call sign is Galana base or if I am on the move Galana mobile, as not only have I got a mobile but the radio in my plane will pick up transmissions if I'm high enough." He asked,

"What shall I be called? It is marvellous that you fly. I would love to do that?" Emily suggested,

"How about, Swiss Peter?" He replied,

"Yes I would like that."

Emily shouted goodbye, as she got in the front seat of the car.

Horatio was pleased when reports filtered back to him about how friendly she was to all the African junior staff. He was sick of stuck up European ladies who treated his men as though they were lesser beings.

Boniface dropped Emily back at the aero club and waved happily at her as he drove off. Emily did not stop for lunch but filed a flight plan to Galana, before she filled up with fuel.

Once she had left the circuit and this time found the cone-shaped visual marker she set a heading for Galana and started to eat her emergency rations. Her thoughts drifted back to Simon. She so hoped he had improved. She had a lot to tell him. She wondered if he would be pleased at what had happened in the last two days. The DVS's revelations had certainly explained his behaviour. Obviously in the past he had taken girls with him on Government work and the DVS had reprimanded him. Emily could see how sporty air hostesses would have loved coming on safari with him. She could also see married women would enjoy a spiced up affair.

Emily also told herself to get real. He had stopped because the DVS had cautioned him. He had not stopped because he had met her. Although he claimed Cynthia was a has-been, Emily thought that if a new lady gave him the eye whether she was single or married Simon would be up for it. Then she was sad, as if he didn't recover he was not going to be up for anything.

Chapter10

Bringing Simon to Galana

Her spirits lifted when she arrived at Galana. All the staff seemed to be so pleased to see her. Abdi had the house totally in order. He said it was much easier getting provisions now with the causeway. Julius reported that they had had some showers on the Northern side of the ranch. He said in a few days they could start moving some of the cattle. Emily set him two new tasks. She asked him to construct a hanger for Hattie. She suggested he made it big enough so two planes could be protected from the sun. Emily was hoping Simon would be coming up on occasions. She also asked him to order aviation fuel for Hattie. She knew it would be cheaper in 44 gallon drums. She asked him to get a pump to attach to the top of the drum so she could pump the fuel up to Hattie's high wings. After a cup of tea and a big piece of cake she set off for Mombasa. She went straight to the hospital. There was one of the other sisters on duty. She had marvellous news. Simon's fever had broken and he was a little better. Dr. Macleod was with him now. Emily sat and waited patiently for Ian to come out. She thought he would be more open with her on her own rather than in front of Simon. Ian greeted her affably. He said he was delighted with Simon's improvement and said he thought he could leave hospital the next day. However he had grave reservations about Simon's convalesce. He said it was vital that Simon got enough rest. He must not do too much. He would get tired very easily. He did not want him to have ANYTHING to do with the office for at least two weeks. He said he had suggested to Simon that he went and stayed with friend's upcountry. However that had the drawback of a long tiring journey. Emily suggested that she would be delighted to look after him at Galana. Ian said he did not think such a journey would be sensible. Emily said surely a short flight would be OK. Ian said he thought on no account should Simon fly a plane in his weakened state. Emily laughed, saying,

"I'm happy to fly him. I got my licence three days ago. I have flown fifteen hours since then. I think he will trust me. It will be marvellous if I can get him in the right hand seat as P2 on doctor's orders. I think his pride might not let him be flown by a woman otherwise." Ian replied,

"That sounds a good plan. Come on we will go in and see him."

Emily was delighted with the dramatic change in Simon. His colour was so much better and he was sitting up. He still claimed he was as weak as a kitten. This was born out at least mentally as he acquiesced to all Ian's instructions and Emily's suggestions without argument. He even chuckled when she said he would have to sit in the right hand seat. He did congratulate her on getting her PPL saying,

"I knew you would sail through that. He then winked at her and said I expect you celebrated by beating up a golden haired god's ranch at Ulu?" Emily replied hotly,

"I certainly didn't." She blushed as she did remember she thought of the guy when she flew by, but Simon did not know about these safaris. She would tell him all in good time. She just must remember in her excitement not to mention to him about what Horatio had said about his possible future. So it was agreed that she would do the radio call in the morning and having packed up a small bag for him, would pick him up, for the short flight to Galana. Ian left and she squeezed Simon's hand saying,

"I have been so worried about you. I am so delighted you are better." Then having looked around to make a hundred percent sure they were alone she kissed him on the cheek and left.

Simon thought to himself, '*I sense a change in her. Getting her PPL has certainly given her more confidence. She might not be the lovely sweet young girl that I am so frightened of hurting after all.* Then he was tired and lay back and went to sleep.

Emily went back to his house. She was relaxing on the upstairs veranda with a cup of tea and a biscuit, enjoying the beautiful evening view of Tudor Creek, when a car pulled into the drive way. Out got Cynthia. Emily thought, '*This is going to be interesting*'. She leant over the balcony and called,

"You must have heard the kettle boiling. Do come up. I'm having a late cup of tea." Emily resisted the temptation to say you know the way well enough! Jonathan must have heard voices as he followed her up with more tea, an extra cup and more biscuits. Emily noticed Cynthia was wearing a pretty, short blue tennis dress with a low top. Cynthia was certainly after something.

Although Emily thought Cynthia was expecting a kiss on each cheek, Emily did not step forward. She was not a great one for girls who were actually enemies kissing each other. To Emily it smacked of hypocrisy in the extreme. However she offered Cynthia tea and biscuits. Cynthia started the real conversation,

"Do you live here now? I expect Simon is still at work. He really does work too hard." Emily thought, *'So Mike is playing golf or something and you thought you would come round for a bit of a romp! Well I have got my sisterly hat on and he is much too ill to romp. I really am a bitch.'* She replied,

"No, (which could have meant, No I don't live here or No he doesn't work too hard, he is too busy bouncing on top of you or actually it meant, No he is not still at work!). He has been really ill with Malaria, (She was dying to say, Oh haven't you heard.). He is still in hospital." Cynthia replied,

"Oh the poor lamb. I do hope he gets better soon." Emily thought, *'She has no intention of visiting him, I suppose she is like me, not much good at the Florence Nightingale stuff!* Cynthia carried on,

"So how do you fill your time? You are dressed as if you have been in an office all day." Emily replied,

"You could say that. Just recently I have been doing a lot of flying." Cynthia looked surprised,

"I thought Simon said you weren't an air hostess!"

"I'm not, it is just that my ranch is very large and as I'm on my own I have a lot of ground to cover. I just came to see how Simon was." Cynthia had got bored with the conversation or perhaps she was worried Emily was going to ask her up to the ranch, so she said that she ought to be going. She thanked for the tea in a voice which said she would rather have had a G &T and left. Emily thought quite wickedly, *'I wonder if number two romp will be available, it would be a pity to waste such a pretty outfit!'*

Emily took down the tea things to save Jonathan climbing the stairs. She packed up a bag for Simon and had a very long shower. Jonathan had made a good supper of bangers and mash with fried tomatoes. Emily enjoyed it, together with the ice cream and tin pears. As she drank her coffee in the fast failing light upstairs, she thought about Galana. It was time to modernise the place. She was happy to rough it, but on occasions like the coming two weeks it would be nice to have some comforts. She was sure Auntie Mary might have had other views, but times had moved on.

She was going to get a generator. She remembered her father on the farm saying, when you are buying things for the farm think big. Always get a bigger tractor than you think you need, you will be grateful in the long run. She now had definitely decided she was going to get a generator and a really big one at that!

She had learned at Kabete that Garissa had power and a water supply. She would need a very little base there. She would not need a vehicle, as she could get a lift in from the airfield. In fact she could probably walk, as it was likely to be very near to the town. She would do all her safaris by air. In fact she was really quite excited. She realised what a contrary person she was, '*Everyone had said what a terrible posting it was. She was going to enjoy it!*'

She was soon in bed and slept like a log. It was not such a hot night and so she was under the sheet she, when Jonathan brought her tea. She was in no frantic rush so she enjoyed her tea in bed. Then she had a good breakfast and made her way to the Veterinary Office.

She was going to tactfully suggest to Simon that he had the radio at home. He would not have to get up so early. Also it would be easier to have a chat in the evening. She also thought it would stop that idiot Mr. Ingram coming on the radio. He ought to just stick to his Port duties and doing PMs on local chicken!

There was quite a lot of chat on the radio, but it was mainly on routine matters. She managed to raise the DLO Garissa and suggest that she came up to see him and have a look at Garissa on the following morning. He had already heard of her appointment from the PCs Office. He said he would fix a meeting with the PC and as many other staff as possible. Emily warned him that they were under orders to get going on a Rinderpest Vaccination Campaign without delay. Could he start getting things ready like; Vaccine, Syringes, Needles, Brands, Ropes, Jablo Boxes for transporting vaccine in the field, Fridges etc.

Then she went to the Airport. She fuelled up Hattie and did her pre-flight checks. She bought some extra fuel in cans to use in case she needed it at Galana before Julius had got his supply ready. She filed her flight plan so that Simon would not have to stand around in the hot sun. She went into the hanger and asked the Chief engineer about generators. He was very helpful. He gave her an address to go to in the 'Go Down' area in Mombasa. She still had a little time, so she went to the generator place. Mr Singh was an encyclopaedia, when it came to generators. She told him her requirements and then before he could suggest anything, using her father's maxim she doubled it. She had expected it to be expensive, but she was pleasantly surprised. He offered to deliver it, but she asked for discount if she collected it. The deal was agreed. Christmas would have the job of collecting it. Mr Singh said he had hoists for loading. Emily said she only had one. Could she borrow one to off load it. Mr Singh volunteered two of his sons to come up to the ranch to do the wiring. Galana was going to have power!

Emily went to collect Simon. He was still on his bed when she arrived. Emily was horrified, as he was very near to tears. Apparently he had seen that the hospital staff were very busy, so he had tried to get up on his own. He had got to the lavatory OK, then when he was trying to get a dressing gown out from his locker, he had felt really dizzy and had just managed to get back on to his bed. Then he said he must have lost consciousness. He had come to, when she had opened the door. He said he was so sorry. He wanted to be ready for her and now he was so weak. Emily put her arm around him.

"I think the best thing is we delay for a day. I'm sure they will let you stay another day." He almost begged.

"Oh Emily, I have never been in hospital before. I woke up and I found myself here. I panicked. They held me down. Then I remembered fighting with you. I thought I had killed you. I am so bloody weak both physically and mentally, pleased don't make me stay here. I'm sure now that you are here, we can make it out to the Landrover." Emily made a decision,

"OK I will help you, but if it doesn't work we will have to try something different. They certainly are busy. I'm surprised none of the staff have come in. OK let's get you dressed. First let me sit you up and see if you feel dizzy." Emily had grave misgivings about the whole idea of moving him. He obviously was affected by the antimalarial drugs. She was also worried that he had oedema of his brain as well.

She loved him so much she hated to see him like this. It was strange what he had remembered. He certainly had held her in a vice like grip. She did remember being very relieved when Jonathan and Ian had arrived.

He put his arms around her neck and she pulled him into a sitting position. Then he swung his legs round and he was sitting on the bed. She asked him how he felt and he said he was fine. She helped him with his shirt. Then when it came to his pyjama bottoms he became all shy and said he would manage. Emily was getting exasperated and said,

"Until you are a hundred percent better, I am in charge. I have seen you and other men in the nude before, just let me help you." He seemed then to accept everything, like he had yesterday when they were planning on him leaving hospital. Emily got him dressed and was pleased that he stood up unaided. She stuffed his belongings in a bag and she followed him, as he walked normally out of the room and down the corridor. She thought, *'He certainly is on a mission to get out of here!'*

He walked normally across the car park to the Landrover. His colour came back to his face. He looked so much better in the fresh air. She helped him get up into the vehicle, but actually he did not need the help. He looked fine, so she ran back in to the hospital and luckily caught up with a sister and said,

"Thank you for nursing Simon Longfield I will take him home." She replied,

"Oh good, take care. We are a bit hectic this morning."

Emily ran back to the Landrover. Simon was smiling. It was as if someone had turned his old self back on. He said,

"Let's get the hell out of here. I hate not being my own master." Emily was backing out when she replied,

"Well for the next two weeks you are still not going to be your own master. I am in charge."

"I will put up with that, Miss bossy boots. You've changed. I never said well done properly for getting your PPL. I am very proud of you." Emily said nothing. All she wanted now was to get him safely to Galana, where she could look after him. His whole demeanour continued to improve the whole journey. He obviously enjoyed the flight. He even looked down at her legs and said,

"No tan lines now." Emily was so pleased. She laughed,

"Oh there are, but I am only white where my body is covered by that very tiny bikini. You were a very naughty man buying that and I was a very silly girl for wearing it. However you may call me Miss bossy boots, but there is still a bit of me that wants to be a sexy teenager." He really delighted her when he said, "I love being with you. You are so spontaneous. I will never forget you using your bikini top as a pad for Leonard's cut eye. I can't think of any other girl doing that." As they were taxiing he said,

"That was a bloody good landing." She answered,

"Thanks you condescending old bugger. Oh look Julius has started on the hanger. I don't want Hattie's fabric to get damaged in the sun."

However she noticed that he was breathing hard as they walked down to the house. Abdi came to greet them. Simon said to Abdi how pleased he was to be back at Galana. Emily saw that Abdi was aware how weak he was as he immediately got a chair right behind him which he gratefully slumped into. Emily also saw he ate very little. She on the other hand was ravenous and tucked in.

Simon did not argue when she suggested he had a rest on his bed after lunch. She told him that she had altered things and now she slept in the bigger room which was Auntie Mary's and where the radio was.

She had a lot of catching up to do, but on the whole everything was in good order.

Together with Julius she made drawings for the generator house which was to be positioned a long way from the houses. She thanked him for getting started with the hanger. He beamed with pleasure. She agonised over whether to bring some of the detailed maps of the ranch up to the house, as she normally would have done, so she could look at them and only wear her bikini, or whether that would be 'work' and stress Simon. She had made herself a rule that she would always wear shorts, however short, and a top in the office. She would only wear her bikini in the house or by the river. She of course was only considering the staff. She was completely forgetting Simon.

Anyhow she thought helping her plan for Galana was not real 'work' for Simon, so when he woke up he found her in her bikini at the big table on the veranda. She had not heard him, so he stood silently just watching her. He thought, *'She is so beautiful. She is really quite small, but she is so wonderfully athletic and beautifully proportioned.'* He was just in his shorts. She sensed his presence and turned and smiled at him,

"I hope you have had a good sleep. You look so much better. Come and look at these maps, I'm planning running water from the river to cattle troughs so that I can water all the cattle every day. I hate it that in many parts of the ranch, they only get water every forty eight hours." She pulled a chair over for him to sit next to her. She loved the feeling of his nearness. She was completely unaware of the effect that, that nearness and her lack of clothes, was having on him. He longed to put his arm around her, but thought that he must not even go that far. In his eyes, she was so young, feminine and vulnerable to being emotionally hurt. He could not work out why she was different from other women. He thought of Cynthia, *'All she appeared to want from him was his body and sex. She then went back into another world of the club and Mike. Emily was different she needed protection'.* He was totally confused, but he certainly was very aroused by her body covered by two tiny pieces of cloth. *'Why had he ever bought the dam thing? He had meant her to wear it, but it should be worn on the beach or sailing, not in the house or moving cattle. Bloody hell she had even taken the top off when she was nursing Leonard!'*

They chatted about her ideas. Simon added new ideas and soon a total plan was laid out. Simon knew how dynamic she was. *'Look how quickly she had learnt to fly. She even had started building a hanger. If only the blasted old fashioned British Government had employed her, think what she could do for the Veterinary Department.* With these thoughts he drunk the cup of tea that Abdi had brought and in fact he really enjoyed the piece of cake. It seemed like the first bit of decent food he had had for weeks. *'God! How he had hated the hospital.'* Then he remembered, *'How stupid and weak he had been earlier in the day'.* He said,

"Thank you Emily for bringing me here to your home. I'm sorry I was so childish and weak earlier." She reached for his hand.

'He knew he should stop her.' She replied,

"You really had me worried. You know when you were first so ill I thought you were dying. I was distraught, but somehow your behaviour this morning worried me more. What were you really worried about. You said that you remembered fighting me and thought you had killed me. Did you really think that?"

"Yes I did."

"Well I have to admit you did fight me. Looking back at the incident it was really quite funny, if it had not been so worrying. I know I should not have come to your house uninvited, but I was so excited about passing my flying test that I was dying to tell you. Jonathan was not about, in reality he had run for the doctor." Then she hesitated and blushed. As she was only wearing her bikini Simon could see that her whole chest was red. He said,

"Go on." She swallowed and continued,

"I heard this moaning noise and thought something was wrong and then I thought." She looked at him and looked away. She felt her whole body was on fire. He said, "What did you think?" She gabbled then,

"I thought you were making love to someone." It was Simon's turn to blush, as he had so often made love to Cynthia. It was their favourite time straight after he got back from work. She was free as Mike worked later. Also she got so excited she often cried out. Emily could now see his embarrassment, but she was obliged to continue.

"I wanted to run away but I suddenly was bold. You had been very honest with me on New Year's Eve. I thought it would be more embarrassing if you saw me running away. I thought that you had every right to make love to anyone in your own house. It was entirely your own business. So I continued up the stairs calling hello. Then I found you naked and delirious. You were so strong. I couldn't control you. Thank goodness Jonathan and Ian arrived." Then she laughed,

"I don't think you had plans to kill me!" Simon was too horrified to speak he was totally lost for words. Emily then went on,

"Let's forget it. You are on the mend now. It is all water under the bridge." She laughed again,

"In my case it is water over the causeway! Anyway you very clearly spelt out the rules of our relationship. I think we both enjoy

102

each other's company. We are just good friends. That certainly satisfied the DVS."

Her hand flew to her mouth. '*Why the hell had she said that?*' Simon frowned.

"What the hell has the DVS got to do with it?"

"Oh Simon, I was going to tell you, but I thought it was best to wait until you were stronger. I have met the DVS and he has given me a job. I will only be on local terms initially, but I'm to be a PVO. I start in Garissa tomorrow. I have been tasked to get all the cattle vaccinated in the province with immediate effect." Simon's jaw dropped open.

"Bloody hell, you don't hang about. Garissa is a shit posting, but I suppose you can easily commute from Galana. I am only out action for a few days and you get your PPL and a job. I thought I had done well and it took me five years to become a PVO. Did Leonard pull some strings?"

"No he didn't, but you and he gave me good references. Thank you for that."

"Right Miss Bossy Boots you had better tell me what's been going."

"Please don't call me that. You make me sound like a nagging wife. I only want what is best for you. Ian gave me strict instructions that you weren't to be stressed and you definitely were not to have anything to do with the office or the Veterinary Department and I go and open my big mouth. Even Cynthia said you work too hard."

"I just don't believe what I am hearing. You have even been talking to Cynthia about me. That must have been a rather strained conversation. I don't know what to call you, but just to put the record straight as we are just friends. You have got a lovely mouth and your smile is breathtaking." Emily could not help it. Tears welled up in her eyes.

"That is the sweetest compliment you could have given me. I will try not to be bossy. So can you stick to Emily! Oh Christ there is so much to tell you. I don't know where to start." She was still crying,

"Let's start with something funny to stop me crying. You are a bugger. No one ever says lovely things like that to me." She blew her nose,

"Cynthia came round to your house yesterday at about 4.30 pm for a shag." Simon just shook his head

"I supposed you told her she could not have one." Emily laughed, "No I didn't, but I did tell her you were very ill and in hospital. She gulped down her cup of tea and said you worked too hard and left. Being really bitchy, she was dressed to kill, it did occur to me she was going to try someone else."

"Emily you are totally impossible, but probably right! Oh what a fool I have been. Can we have tea? I think I need something. I imagine alcohol is not a good idea."

"It isn't just for a few days. I will just give Abdi a shout."

Once he had got his cup of tea and also started to eat some cake, much to Emily's pleasure, Simon said,

"Now what really happened, when I was in hospital?" Emily told he him the whole story. He was very alarmed, when she said she had flown up to El Wak.

"Oh Emily, you must be careful. Please get more experience before you take these massive flights." When she told him about crossing the border on her own, he grabbed her hand. He only smiled when she told him she was worth a thousand camels. When she told him about the threat that they were going to shoot her, he looked really grim and said,

"Oh Emily thank goodness you are safe. Life is very cheap up in the NFD. They might joke, but they do shoot people." When she told him about ringing the DVS he said,

"You did just the right thing. I like and respect Horatio, but he is a hard task master and he does not forgive mistakes in a hurry. You did wonderfully well flying up to Wilson. However you were lucky. Always remember the danger of low stratus on those Machakos Hills. Perhaps golden boy is sensible not flying?"

Emily had to edit her conversation with the DVS. She was very careful not to mention about Simon's possible promotion. However she could not resist asking him if the DVS had warned him about taking girls on government safaris. He hung his head and just said,

"I was a bloody fool." Then Simon asked,

"Did he ask about our relationship?" Emily replied,

"I told him the truth and left it at that. Anyway I'm a PVO now so we can definitely go on safari together. We have neighbouring provinces. I suppose I should apologise for taking over some of your work. Anyway you work too hard. You will now have more time to romp with Cynthia, but you must make sure it is not in working hours!"

"You are a little minx." Simon went to stand, but flopped back into his chair saying,

"I was going to throw you in the Galana, but I am so bloody weak I can hardly stand. I got up too quickly and feel dizzy." Emily was then all contrite,

"Simon I'm sorry. It was naughty of me to tease you." Then she looked him in the eye and said,

"You know I am very fond of you. They say you only tease people you like. You don't really think I'm a minx do you?"

"No I don't and what's so galling is, I deserve your teasing. Come on help me to my feet and let's go down the few steps to your swimming pool together." She helped him to get up slowly and put her arm around his waist. He put his arm over her shoulder. They slowly went down the steps. She looked up at him saying,

"I don't think you are weak at all. It is just a ruse to throw me in!" He replied,

"Now would I do that?"

However she knew that he really was weak. She hoped to goodness that he wouldn't have a relapse. However he seemed OK. They had an early supper and he got himself to the bathroom and into bed. She called to him as she got into her bed.

"Shout if you need me in the night." He replied,

"Now that's an invitation?" She called back,

"I didn't mean it like that you old rogue." She heard him chuckle and she was pretty sure he soon went to sleep. Sleep did not come very quickly to her. She wondered if he ever would want her in the night."

Chapter 11

Problems in Garissa District

Abdi brought in her tea in the morning and then came in again to whisper that 'the Bwana' was still asleep. Emily whispered back in Swahili,

"We will let him sleep. I will go down to the office. Can you call me when he wakes?"

Life went on at Galana as normal. However the new projects increased the pace of work. Emily's enthusiasm rubbed off on all the staff. She knew that the place would never be the same again, when the generator arrived and was up and running. She worried that maybe everyone would not be so happy, but she consoled herself that if Africa had stayed as it was sixty years ago, not only would the people be dying of smallpox but also the cattle would be dying of Rinderpest. She was a little sad, when she walked back for breakfast. The real losers were the game animals. Then her spirits lightened, as she thought how at least Galana was a buffer for Tsavo Game Park from the poachers coming in from the North.

Simon was still asleep. She stood watching him softly breathing. She suspected his kikoi had slipped off and that he was naked under the sheet. She had a great desire to strip and crawl in with him. Was she oversexed? Of course she wasn't. He was a good looking guy. She was totally normal except of course at this moment in time he was still very weak, a romp would certainly be to too much for him. She longed just to lie with him and stroke him. He stirred and woke. He saw her standing there and smiled at her. He said,

"Would you have come in the night if I had called?"

"Of course I would, but if I thought you had been shaming. I would have told you not to be a naughty boy and go back to sleep!" He just smiled. She was sure he knew that was a lie.

They had breakfast together and then she left for Garissa leaving strict instructions that he must stay on the veranda and not do ANYTHING strenuous. He gave a cheeky smile,

"Even if Cynthia calls round?"

"PARTICULARLY if Cynthia calls!" She playfully punched him on his tummy. He heard her saying to Abdi she would be back for a very late lunch. He shouted out,

"Take emergency supplies." She came running back in. Stuck her tongue out at him and ran off again. The short run had brought colour to her cheeks and he thought she looked even lovelier. He heard the plane start, taxi and then it took off. He worried about her as she had so little experience, but at least the weather was good. He thought, *'The only way to get experience was to fly.'* He remembered when he was learning, he used to fly really low on Diani Beach to see if there were any air hostesses sun bathing!

Mr. Matua, the DLO must have been listening out for her, as he came the half mile to the airstrip in his Landrover to pick her up. He had a driver called Chaiko. They both jumped out of the vehicle to greet her. Then Mr. Matua went to get in the middle seat. Emily made them both laugh as in Swahili she told them with a very straight face that Mr. Landrover had especially designed the middle seat for her as she was so small. They both laughed as she hopped up and sat between them.

They went and met the PC and then the DC and finally the DO. It was all in strict protocol. They all seemed pleased to see her. She suspected that any new face in a remote place like Garissa would be welcome. The PC was concerned that they did not have a house for her. She reassured him that she could easily commute from Galana in the meantime. Secretly she was delighted as she wanted to be at home with Simon as much as possible in the next two weeks.

Garissa had little to recommend it. Because there was so little rain the roads were good murram which was a blessing. The water came from wells near to the Tana River. The river and its bridge dominated the dusty town. Emily noticed that most of the few cattle in the town had the Z brand of Rinderpest vaccination. She knew that Rinderpest had a long period of maternal immunity. This was the immunity passed on from the mother to the calf in the colostrum, the very first milk to be drunk after birth. This immunity could protect

107

the calf for up to nine months and make the vaccine not effective. Therefore during a Rinderpest Vaccination campaign every animal without the Z brand was vaccinated. Only animals definitely over nine months of age were branded. The younger animals not branded would be vaccinated the following year and then branded then. The vaccine was a very effective vaccine when administered in this way.

At the District Veterinary Office, Emily was shown Mr. Matua's thorough preparations. She was impressed. She even saw that he had vaccine in the fridge. She went over his plans for the campaign in his district. It was obviously a well thought out campaign. He asked,

"When should we start the campaign?" She replied,

"The DVS wants all the cattle covered as soon as possible. He has extra funds available. How about starting on the nearby cattle tomorrow? Then the Chiefs further away will have time to organise their owner's."

She wanted to make it sound as if the urgency for the campaign was because of the availability of funds, not because of her findings at El Wak. The DLO agreed to start the following day. He said that he would then urgently need further supplies of vaccine, needles and syringes. Emily said that would not be a problem. She explained about Swiss Peter. She would get him to come up as soon as possible. There was little more for her to do, so she got him to drop her back at her plane. Thus she was home at Galana much sooner than she had planned. She was surprised as, when she got to the house; Simon was asleep in a chair on the veranda and had not heard the plane. Actually she was pleased, as he obviously needed real rest. She left him sleeping and whispered to Abdi that they would stick to the original plan and have a late lunch. She did ask that someone would come down to the ranch office to tell her if Simon woke. She did not want him walking down, as she was worried it would exhaust him. She got on with some office work.

When she was seriously hungry she walked up to the house. She was surprised that he was still asleep. He must have been totally exhausted. However she decided to wake him gently, as she was concerned that he would not sleep that night.

She leant down to him and brushed his cheek with her lips. His eyes flickered open. He gently reached up and stroked the inside of her thigh. She whispered to him,

"It was worth flying all around the NFD for that stroke!" He moved his hand quickly away, as if it had touched a hot coal. She added,

"Surely that is allowed now I'm a PVO?" He replied rather sadly,

"I should not have done that. The reasons I told you on New Year's Night still stand. I must not be weak." She gently ruffled his hair saying,

"I think I understand. I can be strong you know. I will prove it to you. I have strengths which are softer because I am a woman. Time will tell. Now I woke you as I am starving hungry and hopefully you are as well. I can smell Galana Curry. It is to be eaten to be believed." She offered him her hand just to help him up." He accepted it. So Emily thought, *'These rules are rather complicated. I am allowed to hold his hand for a purpose. However I don't think I am allowed to hold his hand just while we are going for a walk. It is not really a sexual thing. It is really as if he must not show me any affection. I think it must be his protection mechanism. These girls can have sex with him, but they must not expect anything else. These rules are fine with girls who have husbands or girls who are obviously going to move on. He realises I'm here to stay and therefore I definitely need to be kept at arm's length. What a shame, sometimes I feel like sex, but in his eye that is way too dangerous. Perhaps he is right. I certainly want more than just sex.'* These thoughts went through her head as she was eating the curry, to such an extent that he asked,

"I'm sorry have I upset you?" She replied,

"Honestly you haven't. I was just deep in thought. This curry is good. I hope you are enjoying it."

"Yes I am. It appears that you completely lose your appetite when you have malaria. I was so stupid to forget to take 'Paludrine' for a few days. Then what I should have done was to take a curative dose of 'Nivaquin', instead of just continued on the 'Paludrine' which is only a preventative. I hope you are taking something."

"Oh yes. Auntie Mary suggested that I took two 'Paludrine' a day and that's what I'm doing. Now can I ask you all about preventative medicine for my cows? You are so knowledgeable I can't think it will be stressful."

So they started to talk about vaccines. They finished their curries and Abdi brought them coffee and cleared away. Emily got up and Simon assumed she had gone to the loo so he showed some surprise when she came back with her bikini on.

"Sorry will it worry you. I was hot. Now that we are going to have fridges at Galana I want to know a lot more about vaccination." She had brought a note book and was writing notes as he was talking. She was sitting opposite him and was writing furiously, like she used to taking notes at college. She looked up and he was looking at her chest. With an impish grin she said,

"Do you want to play with your present?" She was delighted as he said,

"And how. Now about Anthrax vaccination!"

They had a very happy two weeks. Simon got stronger and stronger. Towards the end of his sick leave Emily thought he was strong enough to come on safari with her. The vaccination campaign was going very well in Garissa District. Mr. Mbogwa had got the campaign going in Mandera District. Emily needed the campaign to start in Wajir District. Swiss Peter was on his second safari to Garissa. He was keen to go further up North to Wajir. Emily did not want him to go alone so she got him to ask the DVS if he could borrow Boniface, the Kabete driver. The DVS was happy about the arrangement. Boniface was pleased as because he was a graded driver, he would earn a considerable subsistence allowance on safari in the NFD.

They flew up to Wajir at first light. Emily did the radio round up on the way. Obviously Simon listened in. He smiled as she was so efficient. Making sure that the radio microphone was not on send she turned to him and said,

"What's amusing you, Longfield?" He replied,

"I was just thinking how efficient you were writing everything down on your leg pad." She snorted,

"I know I look ridiculous but it is way too hot to wear trousers." She took off her leg pad, saying,

"Satisfied!" Then it was her turn to smile.

"I think you are very much better and in fact you would like to stroke my thigh?" He went red. She continued,

"It is way too hot to join the 'Mile High Club' and any way that sort of exertion might cause you to have a relapse!" Simon went extremely red. She had read his mind! They went on for some time in silence. Eventually Simon broke the silence.

"I'm a little worried that you are a mind reader." She quipped,

"You mean I am a witch? I think I will leave that honour to Cynthia." She continued,

"Now I'm just being a bitch. Has it ever occurred to you that I might be a little frustrated like her?" He scowled. She regretted saying that. She knew she had gone too far.

"Sorry I should not have said that. I over stepped our boundaries. Can we forget this whole conversation? I'm sorry. I do know you are being kind. Can I say that I have really enjoyed these last few days. You have been great company and I have learnt a lot."

This cleared the air and it was a happy couple who touched down at Wajir. The DLO Mr. Kimani had heard the plane and he had driven out to meet them. Obviously veterinary visitors were rare and he seemed genuinely pleased to see them. As protocol demanded they called to see the DC. He thanked them for coming and then asked them all about the proposed vaccination campaign. Emily let Mr. Kamani do the talking. However she could see that something was worrying the DC. Eventually he came out with his concerns. He said that last year he felt that the campaign had not gone as well as he would have liked. He said it was no fault of Mr. Kimani, as he only arrived after the campaign had finished.

Simon then remembered that the previous DLO was a drunkard and had been replaced. However he did not like to say anything, as he felt he would be undermining Emily. Once again it was as if she had read his mind. She took over saying,

"Mr. Kamani and I are both new to your district. We both will value your input throughout the campaign. Would it be helpful with rather that a monthly report, as is normal, we submitted a weekly report. Then if you are concerned about anything you will have the most update information at your finger tips. Naturally Mr. Kamani and I would be grateful if you have any concerns that you bring them to us in the first instance. However we will not be upset, if you go straight to the PC or indeed straight to the President's Office. The Veterinary Department want to get this campaign right. I know my

Director has his eye on me. I can assure you I want to get it right."
The DC responded,

"That will be most helpful. Thank you."

By the time they got back to the District Veterinary Office, Swiss Peter arrived having camped on the way somewhere North of Garissa. The DLO was delighted with all the vaccine and the stores. He showed them all his plans which seemed to Emily and Simon to be excellent. It had all gone so well that Emily thought there was no need for Simon and her to stay. However she was worried that another long flight would be too exhausting for Simon. He was adamant that he was fine and so they said their goodbyes and set off. Peter was going to stay for the first three days to help Mr. Kamani get the campaign under way.

As soon as they had set a heading for home but were still climbing, Simon said, "You were marvellous. I could kick myself I had totally forgotten the previous DLO was a drunkard. I think he got the sack. He was certainly disciplined and moved out of the area. I should have warned you. I did not want to say anything at the meeting, as I thought it would undermine your authority. However you picked up on the problem brilliantly." Emily smiled,

"Perhaps I am a witch. You take over flying this broom-stick and I will have a little sleep. We started way to early this morning." She pushed back her seat and was soon asleep. Simon realised not only that she was tired, but that long flights and difficult meetings took a lot out of her. If only he could help her more. He certainly felt fully recovered now. He just found it so difficult. He longed to protect her, but he was well aware that she did not want that. He really admired her. She wanted to do her own thing. He must try and be there for her, but he was well aware of the dangers. He felt terribly old. Perhaps he was not fully recovered after all.

Emily woke only when Simon cut the revs as he came into land. She stretched. He glanced at her, arching her body, then he had to concentrate as he landed. As he taxied Hattie, Emily said

"Thank you so much for flying I feel well rested now. After a cup of tea with some cake, are you up to a walk by the river and then a swim?"

"Yes that would be lovely. I would enjoy that."

Simon had a premonition that he would not visit Galana for some time. He stored the lovely vision of Emily in her bikini by the pool in his brain. They had a quiet friendly evening and they called to each other as they got into bed.

After a good breakfast, Emily flew him back to Mombasa. They both did the radio round up. There seemed to be masses of problems on the coast and on the stock route. All was fine in the North Eastern Province. Simon sighed,

"I am back to work with a vengeance. Heavens knows what has happened to that fool Ingram. I want him to send a car to pick me up. They were on finals, when at last Simon could raise him. Ingram said,

"He was not sure if a car was available." Simon snapped,

"I did not make myself clear any vehicle will be fine." He replied,

"Then a Landrover will do?" Simon sighed again,

"Yes a Landrover will be fine!"

Simon waited with Emily while she filled Hattie with fuel. Then he said,

"Don't wait. I was well rested and recovered until I came on that bloody radio." Emily took the bull by the horns.

"Wouldn't it be easier if you had a radio at home?" She expected rejection, but got,

"That's a bloody good idea. Why didn't I think of that? Can I call you tonight at 8 pm?"

"I would love that." Emily looked around to make sure the Landrover had not arrived. She gave him a hug saying,

"Keep safe."

"You too, thank you for everything." He touched her arm and walked towards the aero club.

Chapter 12

Problems With the Somalis

While Simon battled to get the Coast Province running smoothly again, things were relatively easy for Emily. She enjoyed their evening chats. She sometimes was really naughty and slowly took off her clothes as she was talking to him. She was longing to tell him, but of course she never did.

One morning the DLO Wajir came on the radio. He sounded rather agitated.

"Somehow the uptake for the vaccination campaign has got out of hand. We have used so much vaccine we will run out of vaccine soon. The numbers are well over three times what they were last year."

"OK Mr Kimani it may be several things. The most likely is that because of the poor turn out last year, there are many more cattle without the Z brand that need vaccinating this year. Anyway you keep going. I will fly up to you via Garissa today. I will bring as much vaccine as the DLO Garissa can spare. I will get Swiss Peter to bring up more vaccine for Garissa today and also more vaccine for you. He will come on to you after spending the night at Garissa. I will stay with you tonight. Can you organise the DC's guesthouse. Have you spoken to the DC?"

"I have sent him weekly reports as we agreed, but I have not spoken to him."

"Well when you sort out the guesthouse. I suggest you have a word with him."

Emily then organised the DLO Garissa and Swiss Peter. Luckily there was nothing pressing on Galana. She packed a small rucksack. She also took her normal jerry can of water and water bottle. She got Abdi to pack her some food for a couple of days. She also took plenty of spare fuel. She set off after breakfast. All was well at Garissa. The DLO was well stocked with vaccine. The Jablo box was heavy and Emily was worried that Hattie would be over loaded. However Emily knew she had no problems with altitude. Also she had used some fuel getting to Garissa. It was the heat which worried her. The strip was long and in fact Emily had no problems.

The DLO Wajir was delighted to see her. He immediately sent a vehicle round to the teams so none of them ran out of vaccine. Then he took Emily into his office and showed her the maps of the district. These showed the crushes and the boundaries of the various Somali clans and the numbers of cattle they said they owned. It also listed the number he knew had been vaccinated last year. Emily could see his problem. She said,

"We still have a little light left. Let's have a short flight over the area. If you are happy for me to fly you, you can have a look at the whole area we are dealing with." Mr Kimani had never been in a plane before, but he was very happy to go with Emily. In fact he was very enthusiastic. Hattie was lighter now as Mr. Kimani was not a big man and Emily no longer had the vaccine. She also had used some fuel. They took off and gained height rapidly. They headed East with the setting sun behind them. Emily was map reading and navigating very carefully. She did not want to invade Somali airspace. However it soon became apparent to both of them that there were streams of cattle, coming into Kenya from the East. However there were very small numbers going back out of Kenya. They soon returned to the airstrip at Wajir. Once she had shut down the engine, Emily said to Mr. Kimani.

"I think that I will have a think about this problem over night. I am tired now and I always think clearer in the morning." They walked together in twilight from the Airstrip to the DCs rest house. Mr. Kimani left her there to go home to his wife and young family. He said he had asked the DC to post two Askaris to guard the plane.

Emily was very impressed with the guest house. It was clean and tidy. It had a water supply and a proper loo. There was an electric stove and a kettle so she could make herself a cup of tea. Abdi had supplied her with plenty of food. Wajir was a very dry place and there were no mosquitoes. The house even had a veranda. Emily felt almost at home. She sat and read a book after supper, but soon was ready for bed. She had a shower. She laughed to herself as the water was quite cold and she came up in goose bumps. She wrapped her kikoi around her and got into a fine silk sleeping bag liner. It was too hot for a sleeping bag. She soon was asleep. Living at Galana it never occurred to her to lock the door.

She woke with a start. A hand was over her mouth. A very English voice whispered,

"Don't be afraid. I am here as a friend. You will remember me. I got my blue in the ten thousand metres." Emily was fully awake now. He removed his hand. She whispered,

"I won't make a sound. Have you come to take me to your father?"

"Yes, will you come?"

"Of course let me get dressed. I think I can see enough to find my clothes."

Emily could not find her underclothes as she had left them in the bath room. She put on her shorts and shirt. She put on her tackies and grabbed her kikoi to cover her blond hair in the moonlight. The young Somali led her by the hand. They walked silently Eastwards out of the town. Emily could smell the camels before she could see them. She sensed more men rather than saw them. She whispered to her guide,

"Will you ride with me? I have never ridden a camel before. I don't want fall off."

"Don't worry there is a saddle to hold on to. I will run beside you. Ahmed will lead the camel. I will hold your stirrup. Emily clambered onto the saddle. She held on tightly as he camel got up. Then they were off. There were three other camels. They moved at a fast lope. Once Emily was sure sound would not matter she leaned down and asked,

"I am Emily, what is your name?"

"My real name is Syd Budra. English people call me Sid."

"Will your father mind if I call you Sid?"

"No he won't mind. He will be pleased to see you. He said that now you work for the Kenyan Government that you would not come. I knew you would, but he insisted I brought ropes to bind you." Emily chuckled,

"What if I had run away? I told you I was quick over two twenty yards." Sid laughed,

"I think I would have caught you after four hundred yards."

Emily could see he was a marvellous runner. He kept up with the camel and they kept going for over half an hour. She called down,

"You sure you don't want to ride with me?"

"You sure you don't mind. We would have to ride very close."

"Come on. I trust you. You could have bound me up like a sack of potatoes."

Sid shouted to Ahmed to stop. Ahmed made the camel 'kush' and Sid got on behind her. He tried to keep away from her, but it was impossible and soon he had his arms around her. She smiled to herself. She should be petrified for her chastity, but she was really enjoying her adventure. It never crossed her mind that they meant her any harm.

Eventually she smelt the fires. The camels stopped and were made to 'kush'. They got off. Sid led her to his father who rose from his small chair by the fire. There was some talk in Somali. Sid translated,

"Father was surprised you came willingly." Emily replied,

"It is only fair, your father wants another look at me and my father will need to count the thousand camels!" There was a chuckle after this was translated. A chair was found for Emily. She sat next to Sid's father. Sid sat on the ground at her feet. He translated.

"My father thanks you for coming. He is pleased that you come in friendship and are not afraid. He is worried that you will get in trouble as you now are no longer a private citizen." Emily replied,

"I lost my way in the dark and Sid kindly led me back to my guesthouse." Once again there was a chuckle.

"My father recognised your plane and he realised that you would see all the movement of cattle. He promises there is no more disease. These are all healthy cattle. The owners just want them vaccinated." Emily replied,

"I will make sure they are all vaccinated. I brought more vaccine up in my plane and more is coming up in a Landrover. Provided they pretend they are Kenyan cattle there will be no problems."

"My father asks what he can do to repay you for your help and kindness."

"All I ask is that he encourages as many Somali young people to come to study in England. I know it will be difficult, but if girls could come as well as boys that would be good."

"My father says he will willingly do that. Finally he says that he is sad that we have to meet in secret in the night, but maybe things will get better in the future. He hopes God will protect you. He worries that you will be discovered if you delay."

Emily got up and knelt at the old man's feet. He very gently remove her kikoi from her head and laid his hands in its place. Then Emily thought he blessed her. She rose squeezed his hands and covered her head again. She said,

"Goodbye and take care." She turned and walked back to the camels. Sid rode with her. They kept a fast pace. When they got near Wajir they dismounted. Sid led her once again back to the guesthouse. It was still dark and Emily was sure no one was aware that she had gone anywhere. Sid whispered,

"Goodbye until we meet again. God go with you."

He disappeared in the dark before Emily could say anything more. She stripped off and was soon asleep. Compared with Galana she slept late, but she arrived at the Veterinary Office as the Askari was opening it up. The clerk made her a cup of tea. She did not have long to wait before Mr. Kimani arrived. She said nothing of her night escapade, but told Mr. Kimani she had given the matter some considerable thought. She said it was obvious that Somali cattle were crossing the border to be vaccinated. She said it was in Kenya's interest that they were vaccinated. She thought that the majority of the costs could come from FAO and so there would be no financial burden to the Kenyan Government. She suggested that they both went to brief the DC. She would then fly straight to Nairobi to brief the DVS at Kabete. Mr. Kimani and the DC were very happy with this arrangement.

On impulse she decided to land at Garissa to top up with fuel and also to brief the PC. She did not have an appointment with the PC who apparently was having a meeting with an important visitor. Emily sat patiently in his outer office until she heard a loud laugh. She knew that laugh so well. She wrote a brief note.

I need a big hug from my hero. How is the eye? Love Emily

She asked the PC's PA to discretely give it to the visitor. She did not have long to wait. The door was roughly pulled open and she was wrapped in an embrace by a laughing Leonard. The PC North Eastern looked on with some amusement. Emily was so small

118

compared with this enormous man. The PC insisted that she was given a cup of coffee. Soon the DC and the DLO arrived. Emily had a job getting away from the party!

Time was not on her side. She had no way to contact Kabete to get them to send a vehicle so she thought she would have to take a taxi. However there was Boniface waiting for her. Apparently the DVS had sent him. She quickly went into the aero club to shower and change. She hoped her fine hair would dry on the fifteen mile journey.

The DVS seemed very pleased to see her. He said he had received a call from the President's Office saying she intended to visit him. Apparently the two PCs had given a glowing report of her visit. The DVS, with a smile, asked why she had not asked his advice, before she had given her somewhat controversial instructions. She did not let on about her meeting in Somalia, but said she knew what he would say and she thought the problem needed a quick decision. The DVS said,

"I will forgive you for now, but please don't let it happen again. You should really report to the Assistant Director of Veterinary Services (ADVS) in charge of the field services. I will be having a reshuffle soon, when Bill Turner retires. I think you will enjoy reporting to the new ADVS." He said no more.

Boniface drove quickly back to Wilson and Emily rapidly got airborne as they had filled Hattie while she was away. She only had to sign the form and complete her flight plan. On the flight she thought about what the DVS had said both that day and on their previous meeting. She was certain in her mind that DVS was going to give the ADVS job to Simon. She was pleased for Simon, as this was a wonderful chance for him. It was a very senior post. She knew that these positions would not be available for much longer, as soon the locally trained veterinarians would be qualifying. The DVS had qualified in the UK at Edinburgh. He was an older man and understood the politics of the Department. She was a little sad, as she knew that she would have much less contact with Simon. He would be in Nairobi. It was a different world from Mombasa. Although she would report to him, he would have all the other PVOs to deal with. There would be no more radio calls. No friendly chats in the evenings. She could see now how Simon would move on into another relationship and she would have lost him forever.

Deep in thought she did not realise that there was a strong head wind. The light was fading fast. She had overflown Voi about fifteen minutes ago. She could turn back, but it would take almost as long as to get back as to get to Galana, her home. She knew the strip so well.

It was now, really getting dark, mercifully she could see the Galana, her river. She had been so foolish. She had been so worried about her possible future with Simon that she had stopped thinking about her immediate future. She saw the strip and swung away North to line up for her final approach, but as she turned South although she could see the river the earth had gone dark beneath her. Where was the strip? She was desperate now. She put on full flap and put on more revs so she was almost at stalling speed. She felt like an owl hovering in the dark. She just could not see the strip. Should she abort and fly to Mombasa where there were runway lights? Then suddenly a set of vehicle headlights came on near to the river. Quickly another set came on much nearer to her. They were showing her the strip. She cut the power, swooped down and flared out. She had misjudged her height. She hit the ground and bounced. Luckily she had the nose well up because the stick was hard into her tummy. She bounced twice more and then she was down. She was rushing towards the headlights. She was braking as hard as she could. She suddenly thought of the driver of the vehicle. He must not die because of her stupidity. She yanked on her left rudder. She could not see anything because of the dust. Her world spun around and then she stopped. She just cut the engine and flopped forward completely drained. She took a massive breath. She was still alive. She heard voices and could see figures in the lights. The door was opened and there was Julius,

"Are you hurt Memsahib?"

"No I'm fine are you all OK?" Several voices answered,

"Of course we are. You turned the plane to avoid a crash. You have saved our lives. You must be more careful we all depend on you. You are very special to us." Emily burst into tears as she staggered out and hugged them all, Julius, Abdi, Christmas and Tuku, her faithful crew who said she had saved their lives, where in reality they had saved hers. They decided to leave Hattie where she was, as they might damage her moving her in the dark. Emily and Abdi walked back to the house while the others came in the vehicles. Abdi said as they passed the grave,

"I think Memsahib Mary was looking after you. Galana would not be the same without you."

Emily lay a long time before she went to sleep. In some ways she was like their mother and they were like her children, but equally they were like friends who had seen her problems and done their best to help her.

Chapter 13

A Lion Comes to Galana

As the DVS had told her not to mention anything about Simon's future to Simon himself, Emily did not mention any thing to him. He seemed to be very busy with both the Stock Route and the Province. He seemed distracted when she mentioned construction of the new proposed stock route between Galole and Galana. She certainly did not mention her desert ride on a camel and her near crash on the Galana strip. Luckily Hattie had not sustained any damage. Emily was pleased Julius had completed the hanger, so the plane was now most of the time out of the hot sun. She was rather sad about the second hanger, as it was unlikely that Simon would ever use it.

She occasionally got a 'Daily Nation'. She gathered that the Rugby season was well under way. She imagined Simon was finding it hard, as he would not be fit because of the Malaria. She was pleased as he did get a mention in one game. Then she worried he would get hurt trying to play too hard. They rarely talked on the radio in the evening. She guessed wrongly that he was socialising. In reality he was just dead beat. He actually really wanted to spend time chatting with her, but he just found radio conversations difficult. He could not see an excuse to come to Galana or to invite her down to Mombasa. He just thought it was unfair to ask her and therefore raise her hopes of a future. He also realised rightly that if he spent time with her, he would not be able to resist her. She was so beautiful and yet so vulnerable in his eyes. He might well have thought differently if he had known about the scrapes she had got herself into and then not only survived, but carried on as if nothing had happened.

Emily was busy at Galana, but the new electricity was a big help. She was slightly worried that she was spending so much money from the ranch account, but she knew she had her local Kenyan salary coming which she hardly touched. She was not really a girlie girl and did not really enjoy shopping for clothes. Any way there were no shops for miles and certainly not at Garissa or further North. She had looked in Mombasa, but she had seen nothing she liked. She was sad that now she had learnt to fly she did not get an excuse to go to Mombasa. She also realised that Simon did not invite her any more. Perhaps he was back bouncing on top of Cynthia. Mike, her husband, had sent her a note saying how pleased he was with the carcasses of her cattle which he regularly bought from the Kenya Meat Commission (KMC). Galana sent a regular mob down the stock route to Mackinnon Road, where they went on the train to KMC Mombasa.

Now that she had started to identify the calves and their mothers, Emily had a much tighter control on the rearing process. When these calves reached the fattening stage she would have an even tighter control. She was pleased that the mortality rate had dropped. She thought it was mainly because of all the disease prevention measures which she had adopted after her long discussions with Simon.

She also knew that now that she was on overseas terms she was getting twenty five percent of her salary paid tax free in the UK. This she never touched, but she just got her bank to regularly buy Gilt Edged Stocks. As she now was an overseas resident she did not pay any tax on the interest these accrued. Her worries about work permits and visas now we're at an end as she was a Kenyan Civil Servant. She mused that all she had to be careful of now, was getting caught in Somalia, neither the Kenyan nor the Somali authorities would be amused!

She was having these thoughts when Julius came into the office. He had just heard that a lion had killed a cow in the night in Kikapoi's boma. The night staff had driven the lion off which they thought was a chronically wounded old male. They had brought in a man who had been hurt and also the dead cow's calf. Emily jumped up and went outside to assess the man's injuries. He obviously was related to Kikapoi as they had similar facial features. He had a deep cut on his inner thigh. Emily knew that if this was caused by a lion's claw it would certainly go septic and therefore she would be wise not to stitch it. She questioned him carefully. He was sure that the cut was caused by his spear as he had tripped in the dark chasing the lion. He was pleased as he said his friend had hit the lion in its side with his spear. Emily got him brought into her office and made to sit in a chair. She washed the wound carefully. She had long got used to the men's enormous genitallia. He smiled at her when she got him to hold them out of the way so that she could really clean the wound before injecting the local anaesthetic. He obviously felt the first injection going in, but he did not move a muscle. She was careful to inject the subsequent injection through the skin she had already anaesthetised. Her small animal skills came to the fore when she put in a very neat row of individual nylon sutures. She explained to him that she had left a small hole at the bottom to allow any infection to drain out. She said that he must stay at the main camp to make sure he did not get sick with septicaemia. She gave him an injection of penicillin and of anti tetanus. She said she would inject him with penicillin the next day and that he should only walk slowly and that he should rest his leg as much as possible.

Then she looked at the calf which had not been hurt, but was now very hungry. It was too young to be weaned so she gave instructions that it was to receive milk from a bottle twice a day and for the staff here to try and foster it on to another cow.

She had a chat with Julius and he had said he would make arrangements, so he could sit up over the carcass that night and shoot the lion if it returned. Emily returned to her work and stopped worrying about Simon.

Emily rarely woke in the night, if she did it was because she was worried about something. She was normally a good sleeper. That night she woke a 4 am. She tossed and turned. First she was worried that she had forgotten to take out the stitches from Leonard's eyebrow. Someone must have done it as they were gone when she saw him at Garissa. Galole must have a doctor or at least a nurse. She worried about the man she had stitched yesterday. Then she remembered the lion. She got up and put on some shorts and a shirt. She went to the gun safe and took out Auntie Mary's shot gun. She knew Julius had another gun which he would have taken from the office gun safe. She walked down to her Landrover with her big heavy torch and some special lion killing ammunition called SSG together with the shot gun. She wished she had taken the bother to really get used to it. At least she knew how to load it and put on the safety catch. At the Landrover she double checked that the breech was empty. She set off to the boma which was some fifty minutes away. She saw lots of game in the lights on the way. As she arrived at the boma there was chaos, shooting and torches everywhere. She jumped out of the Landrover, leaving the lights on, loaded the gun, and ran to where the noise was coming from. To her horror she saw the lion in a rampant position over a man. Other men were stabbing it with their spears. Without hesitation she ran at the lion with the gun across her chest. She tripped and must have released the safety catch because she discharged both barrels simultaneously. The gun kicked violently and the butt went into her tummy. She could not breathe. She was aware of Kikapoi lifting her up and pushing her head between her legs. Then she took a deep breath. As he lifted her back up to pump her again, she managed to croak,

"Look out for the lion. I'm OK." He pumped her head down between her knees again saying,

"The lion is dead Memsahib. You have shot it." He let her come up for more air,

"Who is hurt?" He replied,

"No one is injured only you."

She managed a laugh then and continued in Swahili,

"You can stop now. I have got my breath back. The gun hit me here." She pointed to her stomach. To reassure himself he gently rubbed her tummy. Emily was not quite sure that this was appropriate, but let it pass. She was so relieved that no one had been hurt.

Apparently Julius had gone to sleep, having been alert most of the night. The lion had returned. It had woken him. It had turned when he had hit it with a poorly placed shot fired in haste and run away. He had fired again probably at too long a range. This had infuriated the lion, so that it had turned and attacked. Julius had thrown his coat to distract it, as the Turkana had attacked it with their spears. Emily's two barrels fired at such a close range had totally destroyed its neck and it had died instantly. Emily was so relieved that she had not hit anyone. Her father and her brother at home in the UK on the farm would have been furious with her. So would Simon, although she had never known him to lose his temper at her or anyone else for that matter.

She drove back to ranch, as the dawn came fully up. She was actually elated, but knew she should not be. She put a note on her pad to practice with the guns sometime that day. Unbeknown to her Julius had the skin cure properly in Mombasa. He presented it to her some weeks later. He and Abdi laughed with her saying now she had killed a lion she could choose a husband. She retorted,

"Well it won't be either of you two rogues. They went away laughing. Emily had been a little bit down that day. This incident cheered her up. She could now choose her man and he would have to give her father a thousand camels. This man was going to have to be pretty special!

Chapter 14

More Trouble with
the Rinderpest Campaign

Simon had got his promotion and had moved to Kabete. Somehow Emily felt he was so much further away from her. In fact although he was, as she had Hattie and he could easily hire a plane at Wilson, it was really an illusion. She was standing on her own two feet and no longer needed his advice which when she had first arrived was almost on an hourly basis.

Simon was delighted with his promotion. He had totally recovered from his Malaria and was enjoying his rugby. He had joined a happy Nairobi club called 'Nondescripts'. They trained a couple of nights a week, played a big game on Saturday and often played a friendly game on Sunday morning. He therefore had a readymade social life. He was not a great fan of taking girls away, to 'away' rugby games. In his experience they soon got bored and also because in many cases they were not very gregarious, they did not enjoy the cut and thrust of Kenya social life. He actually thought Emily would be different, but she had her life now. He did not want to rock the boat. He did not trust himself. He was sure he would not be able to leave her alone if she came to stay with him. If she came with him to an 'away' game, they would be treated as a couple. She was so damn sexy. How could he stop himself? He never stopped dreaming about her in her bikini. So he did not contact her. Occasionally they met at Kabete. He knew she stayed with Swiss Peter if she stopped over at Kabete, but normally she dashed home to Galana. He could not blame her. He thought it was a magical place. He knew she never had a dull moment. In the office he was heartily sick of the DVS singing her praises. Simon was cross with himself for being jealous. Others at the vet labs also spoke highly of her. If they ever needed samples from any species they knew she was the one to turn to. She was the type of person who never left any task for tomorrow. She was a big favourite where the junior staff were concerned. She always knew all about their wives and families.

Today he was pleased as she had come to ask his advice about three things.

The first was a problem he had wanted to solve ever since he had worked with the LMD. This was testing cattle for CBPP. It was a problem close to his heart. At the present time, The Veterinary Department took serious risks allowing the LMD to bring cattle down to their holding grounds nearer to the settled areas of the country. These risks were minimal for animals destined for immediate slaughter. However LMD wanted to sell on the majority of these cattle to ranchers to gain condition before slaughter. They had to be tested to make sure they were free of CBPP. This was a laborious business. It required the animals to be carefully identified and have blood taken from them. This had to go to Kabete. Any positives had to go for immediate slaughter. Only then were the negatives allowed to be sold to ranchers.

Emily had read that there was now a test which required only a drop of blood. If they could set up a mobile laboratory, then the cattle could be tested far up North. Then the positives could be trucked down for immediate slaughter. The negatives could then be walked down, tested again on the holding grounds, to be a hundred percent safe and then sold to ranchers. Emily was sure Simon could get the funds through the DVS from FAO in the same way that she got her funds for the Rinderpest Campaign. Emily also said that she thought Swiss Peter was underutilised and he could be tasked to set up the whole scheme. Simon exclaimed without thinking,

"That is a marvellous idea. I'm so delighted I could kiss you!" Emily who was thinking, '*I wish you would,*' replied in a rather dejected voice,

"Sadly you probably feel that would be inappropriate!" Simon quietly replied,

"Sorry, yes you are right. What was I thinking about?"

To hide her sadness Emily carried on with her next question. It was about holding pens and races. She said she knew the DVS definitely had the funds from FAO to purchase two cattle crushes, with gates which linked together and which could be also linked to other gates to form holding pens. These could be carried on a

128

Bedford 4 X 4 lorry. She stressed that the villagers and cattle owners still should build wooden crushes, but in cases where cattle need to be vaccinated in an emergency this system which could be stored at Kabete, could be used. Simon liked this idea. He said he was interested in cattle crushes and so he would look into and source the set-up.

Emily gave a rueful smile and said,

"She was shy to ask, but would he come to Galana officially and help her design and make the stock route from Galole to the Colin's Causeway?" She quickly added, "When the rugby season was finished." Simon smiled and replied,

"I am also a little shy, but I love that idea. I am actually playing at home tomorrow. I would be delighted if you could come to watch." Emily who never really bothered with weekends at Galana replied,

"I would love to. I know girls can be a pain at games so I will make my own way to 'Nondescripts'. I know Swiss Peter won't mind me staying for an extra night."

There was then an awkward silence. Emily got up and said, "I will leave you to your work. Thank you for your help and advice."

Simon was silent as she went out. He longed to say, *'Please come and stay with me, but he knew that would probably be disastrous.'*

Emily did not know whether she was pleased or not. On balance she was pleased, but really she wanted him to have asked her for the party after the game and even better if he had asked her to stay.

She came to the game and walked on her own over from the car park at 'Parklands'. Her timing was just right. She mingled with the crowd. She knew a few faces, but no one really to talk to. She suddenly became shy. She wished she had not accepted and not come. She realised her problem. She did not know the form and she did not want to do anything to embarrass Simon. In other circumstances she would have chatted to complete strangers without turning a hair.

However it was a good game to watch and she thought she would enjoy looking at thirty fit young men. Somehow she only had eyes for Simon. When towards the end of the game, he scored, one girl standing near her said to her friend,

"That's Simon Longfield, he is brilliant, and I am going out to supper with him tonight." What Emily did not know was that actually she was going out to supper with a group, one of whom was Simon. She had not got a date with Simon. In fact Simon did not even know her name. Emily turned and walked sadly away. Therefore she did not see what happened when the opposition kicked off after 'Nondescripts' had converted the try. Simon had caught the high ball, he had been tackled and somehow a sharp stud had opened his cheek to the bone. It was full time. The referee blew the final whistle. Simon walked off with blood pouring from his face. A gushing woman said,

"I will get an ambulance." Simon snapped,

"No way, Emily the vet will sort it out."

So it was that Emily heard over the tannoy, as she was getting in to the Landrover,

"Would Emily, the vet, come to the home team dressing room a player needs urgent medical attention." She smiled and thought, *'This is probably a prank but I'm up for that!'*

She grabbed her veterinary bag and walked back to the clubhouse. She had got her confidence back. She walked boldly into the club house. She heard the man on the tannoy again and saw him in the corner by the bar. She walked over,

"I'm Emily. How can I help?" He replied,

"Thank goodness I have found you. One of our players has a very bad cut on his cheek. He refused to go to hospital and said that I was to get you. I should go straight into the changing room."

Emily's heart sank. He did not sound like a prankster. She walked to where he had directed her. She walked straight in. She nearly tripped over a crate of beer. A man holding a towel across his body said,

"How can I help you, young lady? Have you been on the piss? We don't usually get girls in here." An older guy then said,

"Don't worry about Taffy. You must be Emily. Your patient is around the corner, bleeding all over the place and making a hell of a mess."

Sure enough Simon's shirt was covered with blood. He was holding a towel against his face. He looked up and their eyes met.

"Sorry to spoil your afternoon, but I would be very grateful if you could stitch me up. I know how well you stitched up Leonard on the Tana." She smiled at him,

"I'm glad I've still got my uses. Come on let's have a look at you."
She gently moved the towel,

"It certainly needs stitching, but the bleeding has nearly stopped.
Why don't you have a shower first, keeping that towel on the cut, as I
don't want you to get the wound wet? I will get the kit ready."

The players made a place for Emily to lay out her instruments.
Taffy who was still only wrapped in a towel came over.

"Sorry I did not know you were the medic. Would you like a
beer?" Emily laughed,

"I think I had better have one, to keep my mind off all you naked
men. However where I work, most of the men are naked most of the
time and perhaps better endowed than you lot!" Taffy laughed,

"You're a cheeky one. You want to be careful we don't throw you
into the bath when you have finished stitching Simon. Anyway
where do you work?" Emily answered,

"In the NFD." He looked down at her legs,

"So I will forgive you for your cheek. I guess you got your tan
working, rather than like most of the idle girls around here who
spend all their time lying by a pool. I must say you've got guts. I can't
think of another girl who would have the balls to walk in to a rugby
dressing room."

It was only then that Emily had to admit to herself that her skirt
was a bit short and that it had never crossed her mind not to walk in,
as she had been summoned.

Simon came back wrapped in a towel. He smiled at her as she
took charge. She indicated for him to sit down with his knees
together. She sat on his knees facing him. Her short skirt, with her
lovely brown thighs either side of his, was not lost on him. As she
reached for the local anaesthetic she said,

"I hope you are going to be as brave as Leonard!"

"I will do my best. Pain might stop my mind wandering."

Emily then realised his problem. She moved her bottom up nearer
to him. She opened her legs slightly wider so that her skirt was tight
over his towel. Although he grimaced, as she injected him, he
couldn't hide the laughter in his eyes. She couldn't stop smiling. She
actually laughed when one of the other players said,

"Trust bloody Longfield, to bring his own lap dancer to the game." There was a lot of laughter then. As with Leonard, Emily put in a beautiful line of stitches. She said very quietly,

"I should take antibiotics and make sure your tetanus is up to date. I will get up and stand in front of you." He gave a slight nod of his head. She got up shouting,

"Where's my beer, Taffy?"

He arrived with a 'Tusker', saying,

"What a pity you have done a good job. I hoped you would make his face a real mess to give us lesser mortals a chance with the girls!"

Emily sat drinking her beer with a group of them laughing at their banter. They were very like her herdsmen, when they were herding her cattle or her Veterinary Scouts, when they were vaccinating animals on the campaign. Simon obviously went to get dressed. She swigged back her beer, got up and waved her hand saying,

"Bye guys. Well done winning." She left, walked quickly back to the Landrover and drove off. As she got past Westlands on the Lower Kabete Road, she stopped and drew into the verge. Tears were streaming down her face. She thought, *'Why am I such a fool. I have fallen in love with the wrong man. I have got a lovely job, a beautiful ranch. I must try and forget him, do my job better and run my ranch more efficiently. She smiled when she thought of her Dad when she was crying having fallen over on the farm saying, I will rub it better. If only he could do the same to her heart.'*

She dried her eyes and drove on to Swiss Peter's house. He was nice bloke but he wasn't Simon!

When Simon realised she had gone he was in a foul mood. He had very little to drink and made his excuses. He went home for an early night. Obviously he could not play in the friendly game on the following morning so he went into work. He was in his office thinking about Emily and thinking about how he could source the cattle handling equipment. The DVS who obviously had been working came into his office. He greeted Simon with,

"Thank you for all your hard work." Then he saw his face and raised his eyebrows. Simon responded

"A rugby injury, it's not serious."

"Well whoever stitched it up has done a good job." Through gritted teeth Simon said,

"It was the PVO North Eastern."

"Yes I saw her on Friday. She had been very correct and got my permission to leave her station. Is she staying with you?" Simon replied,

"No she is staying with Swiss Peter. She did come with a few problems."

Simon then told the DVS what Emily had discussed with him on Friday. The DVS nodded sagely and agreed they were good ideas. He said he could easily get funds for the Mobile CBPP testing unit and the cattle handling equipment. He said he did not want Galana Ranch to fund the stock route as it should be government project. He said he would put pressure on the Head of LMD to fund it. He ended by saying he left it up to Simon, whether he got someone from LMD to do the ground work, or he did himself.

After he left Simon mused, *'How enjoyable it would be dong the project with Emily. Then he remembered his reaction to her in the changing room. There was no way he could share a tent with her alone out in the bush, miles from civilisation. He remembered the feel of those lovely brown thighs. She had been so clever feeling his problem and protecting his modesty.'*

He touched his face. She had been so gentle it was not at all sore. Then he got back to work.

Simon and the DVS were not the only Senior Veterinary Staff working that Sunday morning. Emily had left Kabete early and now was flying to Garissa. She had been going to go to Galana, but the DLO Garissa had come on the radio hoping he would catch Emily. He said he had a problem which he could not discuss on the radio. Emily had said,

"I'm airborne and will divert and come and see you. Put the kettle on."

He was at the strip in his Landrover waiting for her. As they were driving to the office, he said in a very formal voice that he hoped she would not be angry with him. He said that he was very grateful to her for coming on a Sunday. Apparently there had been trouble at Ijara last night. He and his staff had been finishing up vaccinating the last cattle when Mr Ingram arrived at the crush. He was with a friend in a private Landrover and they both had guns. They were shooting Guinea fowl. Emily knew there were rare Forest Guinea fowl in that

133

area. Mr. Matua said that Mr Ingram was angry because he had just come back from North of Ijara and said he had seen newly branded cattle moving towards Somalia. Then he accused me of vaccinating Somali cattle illegally. He suggested I was doing it for money. He said he was going to report me. He then left and went towards Lamu.

Emily rubbed her chin in thought. She eventually said,

"You did just the right thing Mr. Matua telling me as soon as you could. You can rest assured that you will have my hundred percent backing. You were under my orders to vaccinate all the cattle presented to you. The fact that they may have originated from Somalia is not our business. I don't think the PC will mind if I call in at his house. I know it is Sunday but I think the sooner that I sort this out the better. You go home. I won't drink your coffee. Hopefully the PC will give me a cup." With that she left and walked to the PC's house. It was the only double storied building in the town.

She knocked on the door. It was opened by two little girls who looked to Emily to be about six and eight. Emily said in English,

"Hello, I'm called Emily. What are your names?" The oldest answered in perfect English,

"I'm Phyllis and this is my younger sister Doris."

"Can you take me to see your Daddy?" Phyllis nodded her head. Emily held out both her hands so they could lead her. Phyllis called out,

"Daddy there is a very little old lady to see you." Emily smiled thinking, '*I suppose I should be upset, but in a funny way I am honoured . I think it a mark of respect in her eyes that I am old and I suppose I am little!*'

The PC came in to the hall. He laughed,

"Emily welcome. Would you like a cup of coffee? I am in charge of these two, their mother has gone to church." Emily replied,

"I would love one. I'm sorry to bother you on a Sunday. Sadly this is not really a social call."

The girls were given biscuits and the PC took her into his study, asking how he can help her. Emily explained the sensitivity of the situation and said she was sure the last thing anyone wanted was a drama in the public domain. The PC was very intelligent and quick thinking. He told her that he had a radio telephone so he could easily have a chat with Leonard in Mombasa, so she was to leave it with him, but he thought she should inform the DVS. Emily thanked him. She called goodbye to the girls and walked back to the Veterinary Office. Mr. Matua gave her a lift to Hattie. He thanked her so much for helping.

Emily flew back to Wilson and took a taxi to Simon's house. She was pleased to see his Landrover in the drive? However she was very surprised went Jonathan told her Simon had walked to the office after breakfast and had not returned. Then she was worried and walked quickly to the main office block. Simon was chatting to the DVS outside the front door.

They both were surprised to see her. The DVS spoke first,

"Simon and I discussed your good ideas this morning."

Emily was a little flushed and was cross with herself. She managed to say in a normal voice,

"I'm glad I have caught you both. Sadly this is not a social call nor about my ideas, but I'm relieved that you think they are good ones. I know Horatio you told me to come with any problems to the ADVS, but I think this one concerns you both."

She then told them what happened at Garissa that morning. Horatio said,

"That bloody fool Ingram. You did well tolerating him for so long, Simon. He already knows his contract is not being renewed. It will be difficult for Chris Taylor being new to the post of PVO at the coast and being much younger that Ingram. Simon do you mind going down there on the train tonight and helping Chris Taylor rein in Ingram? Emily chipped in,

"I would fly you down, but we would run out of light." Simon laughed,

"Certainly I will go down on the train. It is quite a relaxing journey. I will tell Ingram that he had better behave. The look of my face will scare the living daylights out of him. He lent forward and kissed Emily on the cheek, saying,

"You rushed off after the game. I never thanked you for your excellent stitch-up job. I was going to ask you out to dinner."

So the DVS walked to his house which was nearby. Boniface took Emily as quickly as he could to Wilson for her to fly to Galana. Simon walked to the motor pool to get the duty driver to take him to the station via his house to pick up some clothes and brief Jonathan.

Once Emily was airborne she concentrated on her flying. She did not want to get caught out like before, when she had run out of light. She was constantly checking her progress and checking her speed over the ground. She did a final check when she was abeam Voi and thought she was perfectly safe to continue. She landed with about twenty minutes to spare. She was so pleased to be back at her much loved Galana. Abdi soon had a good supper ready for her. It was only as she was drinking her coffee that she thought about what Simon had said. She knew he was not a liar. He really did mean he was going to ask her out last night. That girl must have been just showing off to her friend. Emily felt a fool for being so upset on the way to Swiss Peter's house. Well she was the only one who knew. She was honest enough to herself to admit that she still had that glimmer of hope that he would one day be her man.

Months went by. The Rinderpest Vaccination was completed throughout North Eastern Province. Galana had received more than its usual share of rain. The dams were full so Emily could utilise much more of the outlying areas of the ranch. Her only real sadness was that she never saw Simon.

Chapter 15

A Trip to the UK

Emily was up at Kabete. She had spent the previous afternoon with several of the Laboratory Vets having flown up in the morning. She had been naughty, as she had slightly over loaded Hattie with all the samples she had brought from Galana and other parts of the NFD. She had stayed with Swiss Peter. He had his girl friend called Anita, from Switzerland, out staying with him. They both were very friendly, but Emily felt a little bit of a gooseberry. When they were having supper and chatting, Anita let slip that she was a little bit bored at Kabete. Although Peter and Anita could go away for the weekends, using local buses, she had nothing to do while he was working during the week. Emily asked if he had any local leave due. Peter said he had a little, but that they were saving up money to buy a house in Switzerland and so they could not afford to hire a 4 X 4 to go on a proper safari. He knew he was not allowed to take Anita either in a Government or an FAO vehicle. He said that he knew the DVS did not like girls going on work safaris.

Emily then had a marvellous idea. She asked,

"Would you both like to come to Galana? I have a totally separate lodge which you could stay in. You both would be allowed to drive my Landrover." They both said how they would love that. Emily then said,

"Peter if you set off in your Landrover tomorrow morning. Anita could fly down with me in the afternoon. Then you would be able to work from Galana. I know the PVO Coast is about to start his Rinderpest Vaccination Campaign. I'm sure he would like some help in Lamu and Tana River Districts. Anita would be safe at Galana if you were away for a night. I will ask him tomorrow at the PVOs meeting."

The young couple were quite excited. Anita said it would be like a honeymoon. Peter just smiled. Emily thought buying a house was one thing, but that Peter was not quite yet ready for marriage. When

137

she was lying in bed that night she had an idea. She had been away from the UK, for over a year. She had not been on overseas terms long enough to get leave in the UK but why didn't she take ten days local leave and go for two weeks in England. She knew a break would do her good.

Swiss Peter could keep an eye on Galana while she was away.

She went to the PVO's meeting in high spirits in the morning. She buttoned-holed Chris Taylor before the meeting. He was delighted with her suggestion. He said his wife still had not made many friends in Mombasa and therefore did not like him going off on safari. Swiss Peter could certainly help him out.

Emily was given a hard time at the meeting by most of the other PVOs as she tried to persuade them to let her start routinely vaccinating against FMD. The PVO Rift Valley who was the only one who had any experience with routine FMD in his province, was dead against it being used routinely in the North Eastern Province. He said that his DVO's had a real headache organising it. He said that the modern up to date farms and ranches in his province made all manner of difficulties. Emily said with respect that the cattle owners in her province were only too happy for vaccinations which did not make the animals ill. She had the CBPP vaccine in mind which was so irritant that it had to be given in the tail and sometimes the tail actually dropped off. She knew that the FMD vaccine was much more sophisticated and animal friendly.

The PVO Central Province said it would not be fair as his farmers would miss out. Emily agreed, but she said although she was sorry about this, she was thinking about the economy of the whole country. FMD never entered Kenya from Central Province. The PVO Western Province had the nerve to say that Emily only wanted FMD vaccination in North Eastern Province to protect her own cattle on Galana. Emily was furious, but she kept her temper and said that she now vaccinated all her stock twice yearly at her own expense. Since she had been doing that, she had not had a single outbreak of FMD. She added that she was sure they were all aware that FMD caused a serious check in weight gains of growing cattle and calves. It also killed calves, but the most important was the disease in fat cattle. If there was a slip up and infected animals reached The Kenya Meat Commission abattoirs at either Athi River or Mombasa then Kenya would lose its very important meat export contracts. Emily had hope that Simon would back her up, but he was silent. She forgave him as she knew it would put him in a very difficult situation, as their friendship was well known. However it was the DVS who came to her rescue. He said he was very convinced by her arguments. He said that he knew he could get outside funds for the project. To pacify the other PVOs he promised he would try to find funds for their provinces if they submitted plans and estimates as PVO North Eastern Province had done. When the PVO Rift Valley Province still made objections the DVS rounded on him saying,

"The President's Office has congratulated me for the courage of my PVO North Eastern Province, in standing up alone and earning the respect of the Somali stock owners. I suggest PVO Rift that you get your staff to stand up to these awkward European Farmers."

That was the end of the matter. The meeting moved on to other items on the agenda. Emily was in a quandary after the meeting as to who she should ask if she could take some local leave and go to the UK. She thought it should be the DVS but she thought there was no harm in asking Simon.

He surprised her by saying,

"I wish I could come with you, but the DVS would not agree to it. However if you ask him I'm sure he will approve your leave. You did very well at the meeting. I don't want to sound patronising, but I was so proud of you." Emily felt a very warm feeling inside. He then added, "Your parents farm in Kent, not that far from where my parents live. I know my parents would like to meet you. I have mentioned you in letters home. If I give you their details, I would be really grateful if you could call and see them." He then, to her surprise, lent forward and quickly kissed her on the lips, adding with a smile,

"You understand that was just to pass on to my mother." Before she could say anything he gave her a quick hug.

"And that was for my kid sister!" Emily managed to stammer,

"Of course I will be please to." Then she added to his joke,

"What will your father expect?" Simon laughed,

"Father is rather old fashioned so he will expect a firm handshake, but I'm sure, like me he would enjoy a kiss!"

Emily was so flabbergasted with this last statement that she said no more and went to see the DVS. He readily agreed to her leave request, apologising that his Government would not pay for her fare. He got his PA to quickly type out a tax clearance certificate. Emily was waiting for Boniface to take her to Wilson and was chatting to the PVO Rift who was apologising for giving her a hard time at the meeting, when Simon came running out of the office block with a Government file, tied with pink ribbon which was the standard way of dealing with confidential files.

"I have been meaning to give this to you for some time." He turned before she could say anything and went back inside. Emily did not think much more about it, assuming it belonged to one of her staff. She did think it was a pity that he could not have carried on with his earlier friendliness.

She got Boniface to pick up Anita and then they called into the BOAC office in Nairobi. She got a ticket for her to return to Kenya. She was not too worried that she had a two hour delay in Rome.

Anita had never been on a flight in a light plane before and as she was obviously a bit nervous, she kept talking all the time. However Emily was much more experienced now and so could do all her checks without being distracted.

They took off and cleared the visual marker. Then Emily kept Anita busy looking out for the landmarks, as once again she was a little tight for time. However there was very little head wind. The cloud was high so Emily could climb. Anita had obviously sent her stuff with Peter, so Hattie was light and responded accordingly. They made good time. Emily had one more check abeam Voi, but could relax as they had some few minutes to spare. Peter was on the airstrip to meet them.

They all went down to the house together. Abdi was not fazed by extra for supper and he treated them to chilli con carnie. Emily smiled at the desert. She knew the ranch had a deep freeze as she had ordered it, but how in the hell had Julius managed to transport ice cream all the way up to Galana. Also how did they know Emily loved ice cream? Emily decided to leave it as a mystery. The pineapple with the ice cream was easily understood, as they were readily available in Nairobi, having been grown only twenty five miles away at Thika by 'Delmonte'

Peter and Anita stayed in the main house that night. After breakfast in the morning Emily showed them the lodge. She apologised with a laugh that they would have a ten minute walk up to the main house to use the swimming pool. Anita looked slightly shocked, but obviously Peter was used to swimming in brown muddy water.

It was only when she set to work in the office that she opened the file which Simon had given her. It was not a confidential staff file. It was just Simon's way of making sure she would only open it when she was alone. It was a beautiful small painting of a Turkana man in amongst some big Boran cattle. On the back was written, '*To Emily with All My Love Simon.*

Emily was mortified. She had not thanked him or anything. She held it to her chest and silent tears ran down her face. Did he really mean what he had written? She sincerely hoped it did, but ever the realist she thought lots of people write that sort of thing and don't really mean it. He had also written down his parents address and typically of him had written brief notes. *Father Charles aged 64. Mother Ruth aged 56. Kid sister Helen aged 22.*

Emily wanted to write to thank him, but for once was totally at a loss. After several attempts she wrote. *Simon Thank you. I will treasure the picture for ever. My Love for always Emily.*

She was so worried she would frighten him, but he had written all his love and it was a very lovely and thoughtful present. She could not face giving him the note, so she put it in a sealed envelope and asked Peter to leave it in Simon's mail at Kabete. She briefed Peter carefully about Galana and North Eastern Province, which he was very familiar with any way. Having said goodbye to Abdi and Julius she flew up to Wilson and caught the evening flight to Heathrow.

It was quite full, but she did get some sleep before they all had to get off at Rome. She was looking round a chic fashion shop when to her amusement she walked round an isle and came face to face with Cynthia and Jack Short holding hands. Emily recovered much quicker than them and said,

"Hello you two! Would you like a coffee, being Rome airport it is bound to be good coffee?" Jack rather condescendingly replied,

"It's Emily isn't it from Galana? That's a good idea. What do you say, Cynthia?" Cynthia was still rather shocked and just said,

"Yes fine."

Emily had seen a bar about ten yards away, so she led them to that. They sat down at a small table. Cynthia had recovered a little but was still very embarrassed said,

"We are not meant to be together. Please don't mention this meeting to anyone." Emily replied,

"Of course I won't. I am not a gossip and I live a fairly isolated life. This meeting is never going to be mentioned in idyll conversation." Cynthia thought for a few seconds and decided to be honest.

"Officially I am going back to the UK to see my mother who has not been very well. I hate flying alone and I persuaded Jack to come on the same flight." Jack said nothing, but sat looking rather smug. Emily didn't smile, but she thought, '*I'll let him pick up the tab. He says he such a marvellous rancher, I'm sure he can afford three coffees.* Emily then had really great difficulty not to laugh as Cynthia put her foot in it by saying,

"Last time we met you had been doing a lot of flying. I keep trying to persuade Jack to get a plane, but he insists on driving down that Mombasa Road at a hundred miles an hour to see me. I am so worried he will have an accident." Jack then told Emily what model of BMW he drove and how he had managed to knock off ten minutes from his normal time last time he drove back to Ulu. Cynthia then as casually as she could, asked after Simon. Emily was on safe ground now. She told her how well Simon was doing at Kabete. How he was actually now her veterinary boss, as she had joined the Veterinary Department, but that she was based two hundred miles away at Garissa, so rarely saw him. She did make them both laugh about stitching him up in the changing room. She could not resist saying,

"You would have loved it Cynthia, all these semi naked men sitting around drinking beer."

Cynthia did not comment, but seemed very relieved as their flight was called. Emily was thankful that she only had hand luggage and so did not see them collecting their baggage at Heathrow. She quickly got on a coach to Victoria Coach Station. She decided not to ring her parents, but to just arrive and surprise them. They had just sat down to lunch when she arrived. Her mother was so delighted to see her that she cried. Her father and brother were much more reserved, but Emily could see they were pleased to see her.

Although she had written regularly to them, she could tell they had no conception of the scale of Galana. The vast number of acres of land, the enormous number of cattle and the staff to run the operation was just beyond their comprehension. Her father and brother were very interested in her flying. However Emily sensed that her mother would rather not know anything about it. They all were interested in the game animals, but her job in the Veterinary Department was hardly mentioned. Her father, who she had told to open any correspondence from her bank, said he was very impressed with what she was earning and saving. Her mother asked if she had been to any balls. When Emily said that she had enjoyed a New Years Eve Party her mother was pleased, particularly, as Emily thanked her for making her take a long dress. However very soon the interest waned and so Emily heard all about the farm and the goings on in the village. Emily remembered then how she had never been awfully interested, when she was at college. She certainly wasn't very interested now. She kept quiet and listened which seemed to be what was required of her.

Her mother was very possessive and was even miffed when Emily was talking to her friends from college on the telephone. Her father on the other hand treated her, as if she had never been away. If she just helped him with any veterinary job on the farm, he was happy.

To cheer her mother up, Emily took her on a shopping expedition. It was really for her mother's benefit, but Emily did need a new bikini and a couple of pairs of shorts. Her mother did not like the shorts as she thought they were too short, but Emily just went ahead and bought them as they fitted her bottom and hips really well. Then Emily found the ideal bikini. It was just as small as the one Simon had bought her and was the same design, so it was ideal, as there would be no problem with tan marks. The really good thing about the bikini was that it had a brown bottom with a yellow and white strip on the front of the bottoms and then it had three tops, one brown, one yellow and one white. Her mother was appalled how tiny it was.

"Emily, you are virtually naked. Anyhow whatever do you need the extra tops for?" The young shop assistant was getting bored and

Emily had had enough of her mother and the shopping. She told the young girl how, in Kenya, she had used her old bikini top, as a pad, to stop the blood, when her friend, who was the most enormous black man in the world, had cut his eyebrow. She had then sat on his knee without her top and stitched his eyebrow up. The girl's mouth dropped open, her mother walked out and Emily bought the bikini. Emily mused that it was almost true. She had only put a shirt on to do the stitching on the Tana River. There was an icy silence in the car on the way home. That evening Emily decided to ring Simon's parents. Simon's mother answered the phone with,

"Hello Ruth Longfield speaking." Emily suddenly lost her confidence and very stupidly just said,

"Hello it's Emily." She thought she had been totally idiotic as Simon's mother would not have had a clue, who she was talking to. Emily was wrong. Ruth said,

"Emily, my dear, I have so longed to speak to you. I feel I know so much about you from Simon's letters. Are you in the UK? If you are, please do come and stay, we would all so love to see you."

Emily was really encouraged and so it was agreed that she would come for lunch the next day and stay the night, as both Charles and Helen would not get back until they had finished work.

When Emily told her mother, her mother in an offhand way, said,

"That will be fine, just let us know when you are coming back." The trouble came when Emily asked her if she could borrow her car. Her mother said she needed the car, although Emily had looked on the calendar before she had rung the Longfields. Her father came to the rescue, saying that she could have the old Landrover off the farm. Her mother tried to object, first saying it was freezing cold and then saying it was totally unreliable and would break down. Emily just laughed and said she would have to get out and walk which would warm her up. So in the morning Emily drove to Simon's parents.

It was a lovely old house set in about an acre of garden. As she drove up the drive she saw Ruth cutting a privet hedge. She stopped the Landrover and jumped out. Ruth came towards her with her arms open wide,

"This is a real treat. Welcome." She was a tall woman and she wrapped her arms around Emily,

"We'll go in and have some coffee." Emily said,

"I don't want to stop you. Can I help? I can see you only have the top to do to finish the job."

"Oh would you? I hate that bit as the steps never feel safe."

"I will go up the steps. I teased Simon when I first met him that he must have thought that I was a monkey as he gave me a wireless aerial to rig up in a tree."

Emily made short work of the top of the hedge. They soon came in with Emily carrying the steps and Ruth carrying the shears. Ruth remarked,

"Simon said you were strong. I can see he was right. What he did not say was how beautiful you are. I know he loves girls with long hair. It must be difficult in the dust and heat." Emily replied,

"Yes it is a bit of a mission. Most of the other girls out in Kenya have short hair. He never said he liked long hair."

"Typical. He is just like, Charles. I could be bald and he would not comment. However I know these men do notice, they are just too shy to say anything." Emily laughed and added,

"Simon has never said anything about how small I am."

"Rubbish you are not small. Everyone cannot be giants like the Longfields. He did say that you spend most of your time working with very tall African men. He says initially he used to be worried for your safety, but now he knows how much they respect you. He says that they are all as devoted to you as he is." Emily could not believe Simon had told his mother he was devoted to her. She replied,

"Simon said that he was devoted to me?"

"Those were his very words. That is why I have so longed to meet you." No more was said, but Emily's mind was in a whorl.

Over coffee Ruth asked about her job and particularly about the ranch. Emily really liked her and said,

"You must promise me that you and Mr. Longfield will come out and stay with me. I would love to show you my home. I think you will love it as much as I do."

"I know we both would enjoy that. You must not call him Mr. Longfield. We are Ruth and Charles." Emily jumped up and leant down and kissed her, saying,

"That is from Simon. The only time he has kissed me is to send a kiss to you." It was Ruth's time to be surprised, but she never said anything. After they had finished their coffee, Ruth showed Emily to her room,

"Do you mind sleeping in Simon's room? It is a bit cosier than the spare bedroom. It saves me changing the big double bed in the spare room." Emily realised that she had said rather too quickly,

"I would really like that. What was he like as a teenager and a student?" Ruth answered,

"It is difficult to answer that as I really only can compare him to Helen, which is stupid. I suppose he was a normal boy. However he was very sporty, but equally he was very dedicated academically. I think he was more focused than other boys of his age. He was determined to become a vet and also he was determined to go to Africa." Emily added,

"Just like me." Ruth said thoughtfully,

"That's interesting. However unlike you he became very hard, if you know what I mean. Nothing and certainly no girl was going to stand in his way. He broke the heart of a fellow student when he left her to go to Africa. I'm sure she thought he was going to marry her." They were standing in a typical boy's student room except perhaps some boys would have had pictures of pin-up girls or rock groups on the wall. Simon's room had pictures of Africa." Emily mused aloud,

"This is so like my room at home." Ruth said really quite emphatically,

"You are very different. You are so soft, loving and feminine. You are not hard at all." Emily argued,

"Oh but I am. I have had to be or the rejection would have broken me."

Ruth sat on the bed and Emily joined her. Emily told her about all the difficulties she had to face in a man's world. Ruth listened frowning. When Emily had finished, Ruth said, "Did Simon help you or was he hard on you?" Emily said,

"He was so very kind. I could not have coped without him." Ruth said,

"He did write about your arrival and your Aunt dying so suddenly. That must have been dreadful for you. May be he has matured now. He was a devil with the girls on his home leaves." Emily replied, "Perhaps I shouldn't ask, but what do you actually mean by a devil?"

Ruth laughed then,

"Being his mother perhaps I shouldn't answer that question, but you are so gentle and caring, I feel you have a right to know. He just seduced them. Had a good time and left them here broken hearted and went back to Africa."

Emily was very thoughtful and replied,

"He was very different with me." Ruth laughed,

"I promise this conversation will never be repeated to either Charles or Helen. He certainly was very different with you, if as you said, he has never kissed you."

Ruth marvelled when Emily told her about Simon being delirious and thinking he had harmed or even killed her. She thanked Emily so much for nursing him. Then she thought she had been remiss as it was getting late and so they made a light lunch together. They were a good team in the kitchen. Emily made Ruth laugh when Ruth wanted a new jar of pickled onions from a high up cupboard, Emily just jumped up bare-foot on to the work surface to reach it. Ruth said,

"Perhaps you are a little monkey. You certainly are a good climber. I think you are a little monkey in other ways. You have a very cheeky and naughty smile." Rather ruefully Emily had to agree.

After lunch, to Emily's delight, Ruth got out some old photograph albums. She loved looking at pictures of Simon as a little boy.

When they were sitting having a cup of tea, Ruth said, "I think Simon was your hero when you arrived in Kenya. Were you a little in awe of him?"

"Oh yes, I thought he was absolutely marvellous. I wanted to be like him."

"It seems as if you have accomplished that. Simon has told us about what a good vet you are and how you took to flying like riding a bike. Are you still in awe of him, because although you have had rapid promotion, he is still your boss?"

"No, I don't think I'm in awe of him. He says I am bossy. He thinks I'm a bit of a witch, as I know what he is thinking. He calls me a little minx when I tease him."

"Do you tease him a lot?"

"I suppose I do, mainly about his girls!" She put her hand over her mouth.

"Can you forget I ever said that? It is unfair, as I think they are a thing of the past and he is not here to defend himself."

"Certainly I will forget and I know this is extremely unfair on you and indeed on Simon. My only reason for asking is that we haven't seen him for so long and I gather he is not likely to be home soon. Are you in love with him?"

Emily looked down and then looked directly at Ruth and answered,

"Yes I am, but please don't tell Simon. I am worried if he thinks that, it will frighten him away. I shouldn't tell you this. I had only known him for a week. I was very wanton and I offered him my body. I promise I am not normally like that. He sat me on his knee and said he wouldn't accept my gift because he wanted us to remain friends and if he made love to me he would hurt me. We have remained friends ever since."

Tears ran down her cheeks. She looked up to see Ruth crying. Ruth put her arms around her saying.

"I just hope for both of your sakes that it works out." The topic was never mentioned again. However when Helen got home from work after the normal pleasantries, she quizzed Emily on her relationship with Simon. Emily answered simply saying they were really good friends and that they had an excellent professional relationship. Emily then said,

"I nearly forgot. Simon rarely gives me a hug, but just before I left he hugged me and said that was for his kid sister." The two of them were hugging when Charles arrived home. He said,

"I hope I get a hug?" Emily laughed replying,

"Simon said you and he normally shook hands firmly. However come on, you are still a good looking old bugger, give me a hug," Helen and Ruth both laughed.

It was a great evening. As they were thinking about going to bed Emily begged,

"Please will you come and stay with me. I have got a little lodge with two bedrooms. Helen. You could either stay with your parents or you could stay with me and sleep in Simon' room. We might even be able to persuade him to fly down. He rarely comes now, as he is the' *Bwana Mkubwa*' (Big boss) at Kabete and seems to work all hours God sent." This statement was not lost on Ruth or Helen. Emily turned to Helen,

"You will be appalled by my swimming pool which is really a rock pool in the Galana River, but it has got a lovely flat area to sunbathe on." Helen added,

"I have noticed your lovely tan." Emily replied,

"I'm really lucky. I just work in shorts and a sleeveless top both at my job and on the ranch. When I'm at the ranch I sneak away at lunchtime and top up my tan for half an hour." She then confessed that she just wore her bikini around the house, which included a long veranda overlooking the river. She laughed when she said,

"When I work out in the bush, I don't know why I wear clothes at all. My herdsmen are normally naked, but for a rough blanket over their shoulders. I think it is because Auntie Mary said she thought we ought to set an example." Helen interrupted,

"Don't you feel threatened by being surrounded by naked men?"

"No I never have. I think because I am so little. I am their sort of mascot. I respect them and I think they respect me."

Helen was horrified about her story about her getting a herdsman to hold is genitallia out of the way while she stitched up a cut high up on the inside of his thigh.

Emily thought a lot about Simon, as she lay in his old bed that night. She had learnt a lot about him from Ruth. She did not regret opening her heart to Ruth.

They all had a leisurely breakfast as it was Saturday and neither Charles nor Helen had to go to work. The postman arrived. There was an air letter from Simon. As Ruth tore it open she said,

"I love getting his letters, but I have enjoyed having you with us much more, Emily."

They all continued eating breakfast, as she was reading until she burst out laughing,

"You can all read it yourselves but I must read how he ends."

I managed to get my cheek badly cut in a rugby game. Emily came to the rescue. It was so embarrassing. She barged into the changing room frightening the living daylights of my naked and semi naked team mates. She got me to have a shower and then, when I was only wrapped in a towel sat on my knee facing me, in a very short skirt. She proceeded to stitch up my face. There was a shout from

149

someone, 'trust bloody Longfield to bring his own lap dancer!'
Apparently while I was getting dressed she sat with several guys who
were just wrapped in towels drinking a beer. Then she left without
me getting a chance to thank her.

Love to you all from your even more uglier than usual son. PS the
stitches were so perfect I doubt if I will have a scar.

They were all laughing. Helen said,

"I am definitely coming out to Kenya to see all these men wearing so little!"

Emily left them after breakfast. Charles held the door of the Landrover open for her. Emily laughed,

"We're you hoping for another hug?"

"No just a glimpse of your knickers, that skirt is delightfully short." Emily tossed her long hair and said,

"You must come to Kenya. My bikini is seriously tiny. You will enjoy it." She let the clutch in and roared down the drive. Charles said to no one in particular.

"We certainly are going to Kenya. What a girl."

Emily was relieved that her mother was much more cheerful when she returned. She did not know that her Dad had spoken quite sharply to her mother, after she had been so awkward about the car. He had said that Emily had made a big effort and expense to come and see them. She would not come again, if she was not given a better welcome. Emily in her turn because she had had such an enjoyable time at the Longfields was kinder to her mother. The rest of the leave sped by and soon she was on the coach going along Knightsbridge to Heathrow. She saw the Sloane Rangers were wearing even shorter skirts. She was determined to buy one at Heathrow. Even if Simon did not appreciate her legs, his father certainly did. She had bought an enormous rucksack, as she had brought a mass of books and purchases from the UK. Her luck was in. She saw Taffy from 'Nondescripts' at the airport. He teased her,

"You look like a giant tortoise. Let me buy you a beer?"

"You are a cheeky sod. You can carry my rucksack and I will buy you a beer." As it was they had several beers. Then they had another one before supper on the plane. Taffy did not want his free wine with the meal, so Emily bought him two beers and she drank both of the small bottles of wine. She was definitely a bit pissed when the lights went out. She slept like a log, but was distinctly hung over and slightly embarrassed when she woke with her head in Taffy's lap. He did not seem hung over at all, as he looked down at her.

"I can't wait to tell the lads what you did to me before you went to sleep!" Emily smiled which did not help her headache,

"I'll tell them that I tried, but you were so small I couldn't find it!"

"You bloody would too. I am not one to kiss and tell, but that skirt is really something!"

Emily tried but failed to pull it down. She smiled again, which was a mistake as her head throbbed again. She had shown him a large amount of thigh but not her knickers. She had bought three pairs at Heathrow with the skirt. They were so tiny she defied anyone to get a glimpse of them.

Taffy helped her to sit up and gave her a glass of water. He offered her two aspirins. She declined thinking that they would definitely make her throw up. However she managed her fruit juice and coffee when breakfast arrived. She felt better and ate her roll and the croissant. She just could not stomach the omelette and beans. Taffy ate hers with relish. They had a wait of an hour at Entebbe. They went for a walk on the apron. She felt much better in the fresh air. In fact she almost felt human when they got to Embakasi. Taffy kindly got her a trolley. He had a car at the airport and brought her into Nairobi. She went to sleep in his car. He thought she had been good fun, but he thought his wife would not see it that way, so he drove her out to Simon's house at Kabete. Emily had told him that she planned to fly herself back to Galana. Taffy thought that would be thoroughly bad and dangerous idea. He saw Jonathan at Simon's house and tactfully suggested she had a little more sleep before she did any flying. Emily knew he was right. She thanked him, promising to come to the next home game. Jonathan carried her rucksack into the hall and made her another cup of coffee. He laughed when she told him in Swahili that she had drunk too much on the plane. He suggested she had another sleep. Thus Simon came home from work to find her stretched out on his bed in her bra and the smallest knickers he ever seen, having discarded her skirt and shirt. He managed to control himself and not kiss her. Instead he gently stroked her cheek and was rewarded with a delightful happy smile until she realised where she was. She sat up, regretted that, flopped back down with her hands over her eyes saying,

"I wish the earth would open up and bury me. I have been a complete fool and behaved like a first year student." There was a cough at the door. Simon without looking round said,

"Yes I think we both would like a cup of tea."

She sat up again and told him first about how stupid she had been on the flight. He laughed and said at least she had been sensible not flying today. He said it would be great if she stayed the night and then she could come with him to Wilson tomorrow morning as he was flying to Turkana, as they were going to try and do something about the CBPP up there.

Jonathan brought in their tea and she started telling him all about her visit to his parents. She said they had been so lovely and kind to her. She said she loved them all. Laughing she told him about his father holding the Landrover door. Simon said he would have to give his Dad a strict talking to! Then he looked down and said,

"Thank goodness he is not here now. Should you put some clothes on?"

"I suppose so, but you are different. This is your present!"

He watched her as she dressed. When she had finished he said with a sigh,

"Those are the smallest pair of knickers that I have ever seen!" She quipped,

"And you have certainly seen some! I bought them at Heathrow actually with you in mind. I hope you got my note. Your present was lovely thank you again." They brought their teas through to the living room. Emily felt a lot better and so they both enjoyed the evening. They sat talking until quite late like an old married couple. Then they went to bed in separate rooms, both laughing at their old routine from Galana as they both called from their beds,

"Good night, sleep well."

Swiss Peter had done a good job, not only at Galana, but also at Garissa. Emily did not have to deal with any crises. At supper Peter and Anita rather shyly told Emily that they had got engaged. She said she was so happy for them both. Anita had to fly back in ten days which fitted in well, without Peter doing any against the rules. He drove back to Nairobi starting early on Saturday morning. Emily flew Anita back after she had done some work on Galana. They got a taxi back to Peter's house. On the way he dropped Emily at Parklands. She walked with her small rucksack to 'Nondescripts'. She had kept her promise to Taffy. She had come to the next home game. Simon knew she was coming. She had asked if she could stay, making the excuse that it was Peter and Anita's last weekend together and she did not want to be a gooseberry and spoil it for them. As he ran out on the pitch he ran by her saying,

"Promise me you won't run off and will come out to supper with me."

"I promise, but don't mess about, get out there and beat them!"

Word had got around about her visit to the changing room. Several girls came up and chatted to her including Taffy's wife. She thanked Emily for looking after Taffy on the flight. She raised an eyebrow at Emily and added that Taffy had said she was a bloody good sport. She said she didn't know really what he meant, but she was glad he was back safe and sound.

Simon did have a good game and they did win. Emily told him, when he came out of the changing room that it was because she had cheered so loudly. Then she whispered in his ear,

"Actually every time the opposition wing looked in my direction, I bent over and pretended to do my shoe up. Surprisingly his attention seemed to wander a little." Simon looked down at her short skirt and whispered back,

"You little hussy!" Emily with an innocent face asked,

"Is a hussy worse than a minx?" He replied,

"Either way, you deserve a dam good spanking. My present is for private viewing only."

She gave him a big smile,

"Fair enough Longfield, can I get you a beer?"

In fact they had several beers with a crowd of the players and their wives or girl friends. They ended up eating a take-away pizza in the Landrover on the way home. As they came into his house, Emily said, knowing that they were very near to dangerous territory,

"Thank you for my date. I count that as our second date, New Year's Night eighteen months ago was our first. As you know there is a certain set of rules that nice girls have to stick to, so that they don't get a bad reputation. At end of the second date a kiss on the lips is allowed."

They kissed. Emily felt his hand give her bottom under her short skirt a gentle squeeze then they parted, both laughed and said,

"Sleep well."

Emily found it quite funny that, although they did not see each other for six weeks and actually they had no way of communicating properly, as Simon was no longer on the radio, that they wrote letters to each other. These were not love letters, but chatty friendly letters giving news and asking advice. They were due to meet at the next PVOs meeting.

Chapter 16

A camping trip to Lake Rudolf

Emily was always apprehensive at the PVOs meetings. She was the only girl and was the most junior. She was slightly surprised to see a new face, Greg Turner. She had only met him once at Nairobi Show. He was not her type, ex army and she thought he was a little full of himself. However he had been affable enough.

She was standing on her own. Simon came over to her? She was doubly pleased, as she thought that, not only it had been kind, as he could see she was on her own and not talking to anyone, but also she loved just the smell of him. He never wore aftershave or deodorant. It was not a very marked smell and it was certainly not offensive, but it was very manly and most importantly his smell. He lent down to her and in a low voice said,

"I thought I should warn you. I have got a new job. There may be fireworks at the meeting. The DVS is not overjoyed. Emily's heart sank. Was he leaving Kenya? She was about to say more, but the DVS himself was coming towards them. He said a curt good morning to Simon, but gave her a very big smile, saying,

"Emily. Thank you for coming so far. At least you are not deserting the Department. You guard our most vulnerable North Eastern Wall. As you know, I am always very glad to see you. In fact, I can say, without reservation, that all the staff here at Kabete are pleased to see you. Now if you both will excuse me I will start the meeting.

Although these were very kind words they did not lift her spirits. Simon was leaving the Veterinary Department. Really the last thread linking their lives was severed. They had been getting so close. She wanted to wrap her arms around him and weep. Her pride prevented her. Everyone in the room went to sit down as the DVS stood up on the dais. Simon sat next to her. She was in turmoil, she so wanted to hold his hand.

She had difficulty concentrating on the meeting. The DVS welcomed them all and said he had good news. He said, "I would like you all to welcome Greg Turner who will be joining our ranks as PVO Western Province. This Province would not have suited Emily. It was on the border with Uganda and was all, very settled, with small, African farms. She loved the wild parts of the country. The DVS continued,

"Andrew Dixon will move from Western and take over the Rift." This was a big step up for him as the Rift Valley Province was the most important province. It stretched all the way from the Sudan in the North to Tanzania in the South. It contained all the big European farms and all of Masai Land. Emily could see what was coming next. The DVS announced that Ian Carmichael would be the new ADVS, field based at Kabete. This had been Simon's job and was the most senior job in the field service. The DVS then said with some magnanimity,

"Simon Longfield will be leaving the Department. I am not happy, as he has been an excellent member of my team for nine years. I will miss his hard work and his always good advice." The DVS led the clapping. Emily clapped half-heartedly thinking. I am losing him forever. Then the meeting got underway. Most of it just went over her head. She was so miserable. She wanted to walk out. Kenya would not be the same without Simon.

Then he passed her a note.

We always said we would go on a private safari. I have got some local leave. How about a trip to the Eastern side of Lake Rudolf?

Emily was even more upset and knew she should be delighted, but somehow she felt it was the last nail in the coffin of their relationship which in her present state of desolation she thought had not been much of a relationship anyway. She wrote bitchily,

What has Cynthia turned you down?

She was heartened by his reply,

No, you little minx. I am asking you and only you.

She wrote,

Ok when?

The note came back,

How about tomorrow for ten days? What time shall I pick you up at Wilson? I will have all the gear.

Emily thought, '*Sometimes I think I could kill him. How the hell can I get everything sorted out at such short notice?*' She wrote.

Make sure you bring a big generator for my hair dryer. I will send Christmas up to Wilson with my hair products. I will fly to Wilson for 3pm. That's saa tisa in case you have forgotten your Swahili.

He wrote back.

I have really missed your cheek. Don't forget to bring my present!

They did not say another word. Emily tried to get her thoughts together. At least there was nothing at the meeting which actually involved her or North Eastern Province. She knew that the other PVOs did not want to mention anything in case they got posted to Garissa! Was she being foolish going on safari with Simon? Would it make their parting worse? One thing for sure he was not going to touch her physically. She had absolutely faith in him that he would not be so cruel, as to make love to her now after all this time and then leave her and Kenya forever. She chided herself for being weak. She knew if he actually did come to her bed, she would probably find it impossible to turn him away. Oh well she did want to visit Lake Rudolf. She knew she would enjoy it. A lot might happen. She did not think the Galana would dry up and therefore there would always be water running over her causeway.

She left the meeting and went to the DVS's office. When the DVS came in, she asked him if she could take some local leave. He said that would be absolutely fine. He said he thought she looked a little tired at the meeting. He said a little leave would be a good idea.

Then she flew straight back to Galana after Boniface had taken her to Wilson. She had only been away one night and there had been no dramas. However there was a mass of things to organise with her being away. She decided to take the mobile radio with her then she could be in touch with them. Both Abdi and Julius knew how to use it. In the morning she was on the radio at the normal time on her way to Garissa. She was relieved that Swiss Peter did not seem bothered that she was taking some more leave. After she had sorted out the problems in the Garissa office out of courtesy she walked to the PCs office. The PC did not impress her as much as Leonard. In fact not many men impressed her half as much as Leonard. However she had grown to like the PC North Eastern and he did have her respect. He

157

seemed pleased to see her and he actually said how impressed he was that she had come to tell him she was taking some leave. He said with a smile.

"I don't think any of the other Provincial staff bother, but you Emily are special. You really care about, not only the people who live in this remote area, but you also care about their animals. You know my dog has never looked back after that operation. (His dog had swallowed a smooth stone. It had lodged in its small intestine. Emily had operated and removed it). My daughters are always talking about you. My wife had to stitch up their teddy bears as she was told that's what you did to their dog."

So a very cheerful Emily walked to Hattie. The flight to Wilson was uneventful. She parked up at the aero club and struggled to carry the heavy awkward radio over to Simon's Landrover. He came running over to help her, saying,

"These hair products look heavy." Emily laughed as she knew that he was well aware that it was her mobile radio." He added,

"I imagine there are more?" He knew full well that there was the battery and the aerial in a separate box. When he saw her very small bag, he raised his eyebrows. Emily said, looking very pointedly at him.

"I did not need my climbing gear to put up the aerial. I am taking my tame monkey with me on this safari." Simon smacked her quite hard on her bottom. She loved it and added,

"Watch it, Longfield!" Simon said casually,

"You drive." As Emily went to get in to the driver's side she saw a red rose on the seat. She burst into tears. She knew the worst then. He was leaving Africa. She got in and got out her handkerchief and blew her nose. Tears dried on her face as she broke off the long stem of the rose and put it provocatively between the top buttons of her shirt. She started the engine and without a word backed out the Landrover. It was only when they were through Nairobi and on the Thika Road that she broke the silence saying,

"Out with it then. What and where is the new job based?"

"I'm in charge of the New Panafric JP 15 Rinderpest vaccination campaign throughout the whole of Eastern Africa that includes the Sudan, Ethiopia and Somalia. I will be employed by FAO and operate out of Rome. My local base has yet to be decided." Emily sniffed,

"Well I suppose your home will be handy for the Alps. I might come and see you when I come on leave as I am now on overseas terms." Simon replied,

"I would love that. We have never talked about the Alps. Are you a keen skier?"

"Yes, my father used to go in the 1920s. He took my brother and I in 1950 for the first time. I was only six. How about you?"

"Oh dear, that is a shame as I did not start until I was fourteen. You will be much better than me." Emily's face lit up. She thought, *'He may be right. I am in fact better than my brother as he started when he was eight.'* She replied,

"I doubt it. Men are usually stronger skiers than girls particularly little girls." Simon grunted,

"I seem to remember you saying a strong woman was a lot better than a weak man. I remember the occasion quite well." Emily also remembered that evening which felt a millennium ago. She answered,

"Well yes, however I am sure you are better at climbing trees?" He answered,

"I don't expect so, if the trees are as prickly as you are today!" Emily tossed her long blond hair, but said nothing. They travelled on in silence for over a hundred miles to Simon's friends, Pat and Derek on a ranch near Nanuyki. Simon had not said he was bringing anyone, so they were surprised to see Emily. They were very welcoming and had kept supper for them. Their four young children were already in bed. Supper was lively and Emily felt she had been accepted by his friends. When they went to bed Derek showed them the hundred yards to a tiny guest house. His parting words were,

"I hope it will be OK there is only one bed. Sleep well." Simon replied in a very off-hand way,

"We will be fine."

Emily's heart did a flip. They had never shared a bed before. Emily was grateful for the dark. She suddenly blushed all over. She thought that she had really been in love with Simon from when she first met him, and he had rescued her over eighteen months ago at Galana. She tried to think in a positive way. He had always really been kind to her and always seemed to be delighted to see her, but he had never showed her any real affection. She had given him a hug sometimes which seemed to embarrass him, so she had been careful only to hug him when they were alone and had not seen one another for some time. She longed for him to kiss her. She loved it when he held her to him when they had danced on New Year's Night.

Wow tonight they were sharing a bed. She wondered what would happen. In fact as far as she was concerned it was a non-event. There was a separate bathroom and small kitchen from the bedroom. The bed was not a proper double bed so it was quite small. Emily hoped he would reach for her in bed, but after they both got in, wrapped in kikois, hers over her breasts and his round his waist, he switched off the light saying the usual,

"Sleep well."

She was sure, although it seemed like a long time, that they both went to sleep quite quickly. Simon was still asleep when she woke. She carefully got out of bed and went for a wee. Then she put the kettle on for a cup of tea. She heard him get up and have a wee, so she made two cups. He was sitting up in bed when she brought them in. She knew that she should have walked around the bed, but she suddenly felt sexy and so lent over to put his mug on his side having put hers down on her side. Her kikoi had worked itself loose. It slipped down exposing her breasts. Their eyes met as he held her kikoi up to preserve her modesty. Emily did nothing to cover up, but keeping eye contact lifted her leg over him so she was straddling his legs. She never knew what made her so bold, but she raised her arms so her pert breasts stuck out in a very inviting manner and said,

"I thought you spoke for both of us last night, saying we will be fine!" He said nothing, but his eyes never left hers, as she sat totally naked in front of him. She dropped her hands to the sheet and slowly drew it down together with his now loose kikoi. His arousal was obvious. She reached forward and wrapped her arms around his neck and kissed him passionately. When they eventually came up for air, she giggled and said,

"I think we will be fine."

Then to her amazement he said, "Emily will you marry me?" She very thoughtfully replied,

160

"I would really love that, but I really meant I think sex will be fine. You don't have to marry me." He replied,

"I have always wanted to marry you since I held you in my arms at midnight eighteen months ago, on New Year's Night."

Emily really laughed then,

"Well you took a bloody long time to tell me. I have been longing for you for all those months. Come on we have a lot of wasted time to make up. Her arms went around him again and she felt him hard against her. Their love making was wonderful. As they were lying in each other's arms both totally spent. He asked,

"Can we make Galana our home?" That was really too much for Emily, she rolled on top of him saying,

"Of course we can you silly old goat." Then they made love again. Emily wondered whether it was symbolic that she was on top!

#0121 - 011217 - C0 - 210/148/9 - PB - DID2050737